Dedication

This book is dedicated to my children:

Wesley
who has taught me to fight for what I believe in.

Regan
who has showed me there is beauty everywhere.

Darby
the Aussie who is the reason why we put deadbolts on all the doors
Zeus

the Mutt who is unafraid of trying new chew toys like our couch.

PS Dave still owns Darby and Zeus.

Acknowledgement

Many thanks go out to:

Everyone who encouraged me to write a second book

The staff at Carver Middle School for giving me such great ideas

The awesome staff at Turnip Press who just...know everything

When Bees Buzz

-1-

Face to snout with her despicable Australian Shepherd.

"Oh, that feels good." Sabine Metzke murmured. She snuggled deeper into her pillow and smiled. She loved waking up in the morning with her boyfriend, Newt, nuzzling her neck. "If you don't stop, you'll be late for work."

"I'm already dressed." Newt called from the bathroom. His Swedish accent was muffled by the toothbrush.

"What?" Sabine rolled over immediately and found herself face to snout with her despicable Australian Shepherd, Dingo. "Oh my God, you are such a little evil witch." Sabine's voice dropped to a whisper. "And wait until Newt leaves. Then it's bye-bye Aussie in the house."

Dingo's marble eyes flickered as if challenging her as the alpha female. Since Sabine had started dating Newt six months ago, Dingo, who Sabine raised from an eight-week old puppy, had switched her allegiance to Newt.

"Is something wrong in here?" Newt poked his head from the bathroom. He was already dressed in his "court" suit. Newt was the only detective in the Jaemore County, Georgia Sheriff's Office. One of his cases was scheduled for opening arguments and Newt was the first witness.

"Why, no. Why do you ask?" Sabine batted her eyes at her boyfriend.

"I heard you whispering, and Dingo looks a little upset. Did you say anything mean?"

Sabine darted a glance to the Aussie. If anything, Dingo's expression reflected a superior attitude.

"She's a dog, Newt. It doesn't matter what I say to her."

"Oh, but she's the sweetest, cutest, smartest puppy dog in the world." Newt cooed at the dog when he walked to the end of the bed.

Dingo turned to look at Newt and sat one back leg on Sabine's face. And to add great insult to injury the dog rolled on her back on top of Sabine.

"How can someone get mad at this baby?" He scratched Dingo on the sweet spot on her belly and her back paws.

"Me." Sabine's response was muffled. Not many people would identify with Sabine's misery. Who else would have a maniacal dog that ran the household and had the man of the house putty in her hairy paw?

Newt patted Dingo's head one more time before returning to the bathroom. Dingo jammed her back paws into Sabine's shoulders before leaping off the bed.

"Witch." Sabine muttered in a bitter tone. "After all the things I've done for that dog and she takes over my boyfriend."

Even when she said boyfriend in her most sour tone, she had to pinch herself. Six months ago, the best part of her social life was shopping at Dupont's Supermarket on a Friday with her best friend, Mia Wallis. It was always a hotspot for police activity that included shoplifters and a few ladies of the evening hoping to pick up quick money.

One afternoon in early April, all that changed when she had to interview Edweener Bumpus for a feature article about the moonshine industry. Sabine had her late aunt to thank for opening the door to writing for "Dixie Days"-- the magazine for "Everything Southern.". In the space of two weeks, Sabine and Mia had uncovered a burgeoning meth lab, helped an alcoholic mother named Arial Bixby be reunited with her children, acquired boyfriends, and shook the Old Southern Guard to its knees.

"Do you want to meet at The Store for lunch?" Newt shrugged his jacket on. "I know for a fact Judge Monroe will call a recess especially MeeMaw is cooking up her five-alarm spicy chili today at The Store." The Store was the only diner in the county that regularly passed Health Department inspections. An added bonus was that the restaurant was within walking distance from every point in small town Greenleaf.

Sabine pondered her schedule for a moment. Her latest article for Dixie Days was about geocaching, the electronic scavenger hunt using a global positioning satellite unit. The Dixie Days deadline loomed in five days.

"Probably not. I'm meeting a geocache named Drayton Wilcox to hunt a cache at the old Animal Safari. He's picking me up here later. And I'm going to start on the article." Sabine stretched her lower back. She mentally mapped her way to the abandoned farm that once hoped to supply bison and other exotic cuts of meat to local restaurants. It never caught on and went out of business soon after opening. "I need to write it because I totally flaked out on it this weekend when the Aggies won on Saturday."

Newt frowned and nodded. He did not fully realize how fanatical Sabine and the majority of the SEC population could be about their teams until he witnessed it. He'd scored two tickets to the Texas A&M/South Carolina game the previous month. After attending the game, Sabine needed a full day to recover from the hissing and singing during the game. The one thing he was thankful after witnessing his girlfriend was that it wasn't the Georgia Bulldogs game. He seriously did not think Sabine and Mia's friendship would have survived if both women had attended that game, "Well, be careful. You'll be hiking and you know how you are when you don't think things through. I love you, but remember the fire ant mound?"

Sabine crinkled her nose and scratched a long-gone welt on her stomach. She had fallen into a fire ant mound while trying to help Mia escape a nosy TV reporter. Her entire lower half her body had been covered in bites. “I love you, too. I’ll be careful. I’m just hiking around an old road and it’s October. The ants are going into hibernation. What trouble can I get into?”

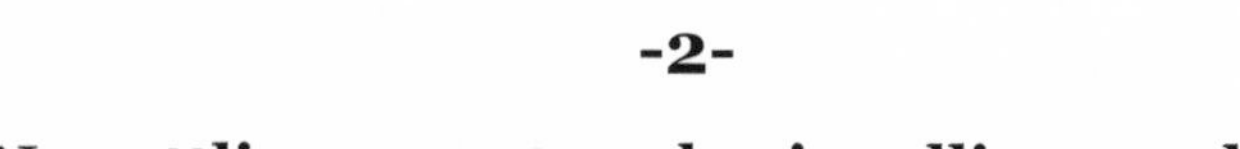

-2-

No rattling except my brain telling me this is a stupid idea.

Sabine grasped the GPS unit with tight fingers. Considering how much one cost, she didn't want to drop the borrowed equipment. She was so far away from her element. Hiking all over rural Jaemore County with her eyes trained on a small computer. There were no other businesses near the defunct Morgan's Animal Safari. The dismal, rusty business sign hung desolately from equally rusty chains attached to a locked gate. Rock walls framed the side of the gate. In the distance, Sabine took in a lonely chimney, no doubt just as abandoned as the rest of the farm. Sabine felt as if she and Drayton Wilcox were the only humans on the planet.

"Now the GPS is only part of the hunt. It'll get you to the general area but at some point, you just have to start using your eyes." Drayton pulled off his John Deere cap and scratched a spot on his bald head. Although it was close to fall in north central Georgia, summer had not released its hold. The humidity was near 100% and the temperature hovered in the low 80s. "You have to develop a nose for it. Ask yourself–if I was going to hide an ammo can, where would I put it?"

Sabine wiped the sweat from her brow. "I don't know. Maybe up a tree or dig a hole." According to the unit, she was standing on top of an old steel box once used to house ammunition for the US Army.

"Naw. You can't bury it where you have to dig it up. But a tree would be a good idea. If there was one around here." Drayton cast his eyes around taking in all the rotting stumps. "Kirby Morgan cut down all the trees when he bought this place. He was so excited. He just knew he could sell alternative meats to three-star Michelin restaurants all over the country, especially Atlanta and Savannah. I told him he was making a mistake. Without those trees, Georgia red clay becomes hard as cement and you can't grow grass to feed all those animals. We almost got into a fight over it."

Drayton's large hands clenched into fists. "He hired me because I have a bachelor's in turfgrass management from Abraham Baldwin College in Tifton and he didn't take my advice. No one would touch me when the animal farm went under. Everyone blamed me for the grass debacle. Kirby messed up my ag career so much that I had to switch career paths." Drayton kicked at an errant pebble that crashed into the faded green desolate sign proclaiming the entrance to Kirby Morgan's Exotic Animal Safari.

Sabine winced. She didn't know all that backstory and felt for Drayton. He was a tall and muscular African American fire safety educator from neighboring Hooks county. Lee Kingsley, Mia's steady boyfriend and Jaemore County's fire chief, had introduced them when Sabine bemoaned the fact that she didn't know anyone who geocached. Her Dixie Days editor, Helen Stanley, had sent a terse email assigning the feature on geocaching with no direction or contacts. Lee had met Drayton during an emergency when one of the Lyons boys set off fireworks in a dry field on the county line during a dry spell last July and geocaching had come up in the conversation.

"Sorry," Drayton's voice boomed. "I didn't mean for the rock to take off like a rocket." He motioned further toward the fading aluminum sign and crumbling rock facade. "I'd be willing to bet it's hidden over there. There are lots of hidey-holes." He grinned, showing blindingly white teeth against an ebony canvas.

"Uh, don't snakes or large man-eating bugs live in places like that?"

Drayton nodded. "That's why you poke at it before you stick your fool hand down a spot. But that's the fun of geocaching. You never know when you're going to visit the ER or find buried treasure."

"Like gold? Because that's the only time I'd be willing to poke at a hole that may or may not have a boa constrictor in it."

Drayton scoffed. "There are no wild boas around here. Listen for the rattle of an Eastern Diamondback. Anyway, most snakes would rather skedaddle rather than go up against humans."

"That's great about the boa and I don't hear any rattle! Just verifying—we're clear of poisonous snakes?" Sabine inched toward the rocks with her hand extended. Well, she thought, no rattling except my brain telling me this is a stupid idea.

"You do have to worry about the copperhead. They are sneaky little bastards who don't slither away. They'd bite rather than run. And snakes are venomous, not poisonous. Believe it or not, I've transported more than my fair share of snake bite victims. Be careful when you hunt."

Sabine's hand froze a foot from the closest rock. Drayton picked up a dead branch and pried the rock mountain apart.

He whooped like a five-year-old on Christmas day. "Yep, there it is. And it's a huge cache. Look at the size of that ammo can. There will be lots of swag in this one."

Sabine still had not moved and had focused her eyes on a spectacle behind him. "Drayton, you don't happen to know of any cemeteries around here?"

"Not that I know of. Why?"

"Because Mia's wienie dog, Snookie, just raced up out of nowhere and is right behind you with a human arm in her mouth."

Drayton's head whipped around to see Snookie wagging her little sausage shaped body with the remains of a skeletal arm in her mouth. She dropped the hand at Sabine's feet and sat waiting for her reward.

"Dray..." Sabine's eyes darted back to her companion only to watch him faint and splayed out over the rocks and geocache.

-3-

Maintaining Western civilization through thank you notes and covered dinners for funerals.

"It's got to belong to Dorcas Priest." Mia bit her lower lip and at the same time, managed not smear her designer lipstick while she made her prediction. "Snookie has being trying to dig her up for a year. And you know how stubborn Snookie can be. She escapes the house so much that Mom bought a blinking solar light for Snookie's collar so people can see Snookie at night." Mia peered over the crime scene tape while petting her errant dachshund. As a nosy, native Greenleafer, Mia had a police scanner in her office at the Department of Family and Children Services. Word of the 9-1-1 call had quickly spread and Sabine counted four acquaintances who arrived before the first responder did.

"I don't know how she escaped the electronic fence around my house. Dad probably fell asleep and Snook took off." Mia paused to take a breath. "And why would she give it to you? If anything, she should have made the trek to my office and dropped it at my feet. I'm her owner, well, one of her owners. She brings me everything else under sun including that nasty chew toy." Mia frowned and reached down to dust a speck of clay off her Miu Miu heels. She continued to ponder out loud why Snookie hated the long dead Dorcas Priest enough to dig her up.

Sabine shook her head. Mia's dog was a handful to say the least. As any true dachshund who loved to dig, Snookie had been trying to exhume Dorcas Priest who died 85 years ago and was presently interred in the First Baptist's Church cemetery two miles away. It was mind boggling, Snookie's obsession with Dorcas' grave. Maybe, in a previous lifetime the woman had been mean to Snookie. Only if one believed in reincarnation for the canine.

The dachshund was tame compared to the rest of the Wallis family. Sabine had been more or less adopted by Micah and Denise Wallis since the move from Houston a year ago. Micah Wallis was a retired Navy seaman and postal employee with a penchant for Sports Illustrated swimsuit editions and crime scenes. Mrs. Wallis was the most successful real estate agent in the area as well as the biggest gossip in four states. Mia was, for better or worse, a beautiful amalgamation of the two. She was a younger gorgeous version of Denise Wallis coupled with the peculiar mindset of her father. The last Wallis, Mia's younger brother, Caleb, was finishing up his last year at the US Coast Guard Academy up north but seemed relatively normal compared to the rest of his family.

At twenty-five years old, Mia was the county's only child protective service investigator for the Department of Family and Children Services or DFCS. After graduating from the University of Georgia with a bachelor's degree in social work, she rebuffed offers to model for national beauty magazines and returned home to Greenleaf in quiet Jaemore County in north central Georgia. Her ancestors had been former slaves who worked in the Underground Railroad before and during the Civil War. Mia's roots were deep in the red clay of her hometown.

Sabine hung behind the willowy Mia when she spied Newt marching toward her. "I swear I didn't give Snookie the command to dig up Dorcas Priest or even drop her arm."

Newt heaved a sigh. "No, I can't blame you for this. This," Newt swept his left arm over the abandoned land, "was all Snookie. And this," he motioned with his right hand at the swelling crowd, "is all Jaemore County."

"What is the protocol? Does Mia have to write an apology letter to Dorcas before we rebury her arm?" Sabine snickered and then brightened. "Does this mean we get to have a funeral reception so your mom can make her homemade cheese straws? I mean we missed Dorcas' original one in 1932."

Mia glowered at Sabine. Denise Wallis, Southern dowager as she was, was militant about following customs and maintaining Western civilization through thank you notes and covered dinners for funerals. During the last spring, Mia had unintentionally interrupted the late Myra Havens' graveside service and had to hand write an apology letter to the deceased. When Mia protested that Myra couldn't read it as she was as dead as a doornail, Mrs. Wallis ordered two notes written—one for the interruption and the other for reminding Myra that she had died. One of the last funerals was for poor Louis Dixon who had the unfortunate luck to have a bad heart and to be standing near a careening Bugatti in the past spring. Mrs. Wallis made her famous cheese straws.

Sabine's mouth watered at the thought of those cheesy pieces of heaven. She mentally shook herself to return to the present. "I wonder if Drayton is okay? When he fainted, he went down like a piece of granite." Sabine craned her neck in an attempt to spot her geocaching guide.

Mia scrunched her nose. "Oh, Drayton couldn't handle the sight of blood or any gore. He passed out during the Winkie Bowl football game during my freshman year in high school. I remember that I missed the sale at Macy's that year because Caleb got pink eye. He gave it to everyone, so we called him 'Conjunctivitis Caleb'. Drayton got pink eye and couldn't see when he plowed into a ref...."

Sabine didn't have the patience for the drama of the annual championship football game between Jaemore and Hooks counties. "Why is he a firefighter then? He's a first responder and they can't have anyone fainting during a car wreck."

"Well, he mostly does fire education, so he stays out of the gross stuff. He's the helicopter pilot for the life flights, so blood, goo and guts are all in the back seat of the helicopter." Mia waved away Sabine's concerns. "He's just finishing his master's degree in business with an online college because y'all know firefighters don't make a bunch of money. I'll call Momma to see if she knows of any of Dorcas' relatives." Mia transferred Snookie to her other hand as she dug around her costly handbag.

"No, don't call." Newt ran his fingers through his thinning blonde hair. "It's not Dormant Pastor."

"Dorcas Priest." Mia corrected him.

"Whoever. Not unless Dorcas had invented medical alert bracelets." Newt place his hand under the dog's face and lifted it. Coal black eyes met his. Newt could have sworn a flash of guilt passed through the dog's face.

Sabine opened her mouth and closed it as Mia stared at Newt. Mia found her voice first.

"What exactly are you saying, Detective Johansson? That Snookie is a murderer?" Mia snatched and pulled Snookie away. "Is that what you're insinuating? Because it's not true! Snook does not have a murderous bone in her innocent little wienie body!"

"Mia, I didn't mean..." Newt braced himself for Mia's melodramatics. The woman was a diva and drama queen tightly bound in her tiny figure.

"Sabine, call my mom. We have to get Snookie a lawyer. I know her rights. I've seen Law and Order too many times. She doesn't have to answer any questions." Mia backed away slowly with Snookie in a death grip. "You're going to have recuse yourself Newt. You are personally involved with our family. You're dating Sabine and she's Snookie's aunt. Call the sheriff. He'll have to take over."

Sabine cut her eyes at Newt. She knew Mia was being farfetched in her histrionics, but she was also entertained by the exasperated look on Newt's face. "Mia, first of all, I don't think Newt was accusing Snook of first-degree murder. Second, she's a dog and arresting her is not in Newt's jurisdiction. Lastly, you're choking Snook so relax. No one is going to walk Snookie down the green mile. Newt can't recuse himself. Sheriff Ostermeyer couldn't investigate himself out of a paper bag, especially after getting married to Edweener this past summer."

Mia relaxed her grip and Sabine heartened to see life returning to Snookie's face. She continued on her absurd tirade. "Just so you know, Newt, I can make your life miserable in Greenleaf. Want to eat at The Store? Nope, no tables. Wanna keep dating Sabine? You'll have to go through my dad. Ever need to be defended in a foreign country or drug runners in the Caribbean? Don't call my brother Caleb! He won't bring any Coast Guard boats your way."

"Wait, wait. What does my love life have to do with this?" Sabine demanded. She swiveled and glare up to her soon to be former best friend. "Don't paint me in the corner with that homicidal canine of yours. I can't help that Snookie is addicted to digging up dead people. Maybe, you should consider putting her into some type of rehab like Diggers Anonymous." Sabine was eager to deflect attention away from her love life. "Newt, can't you arrest Mia for not keeping her dog in her yard? Or maybe as an accessory to disturbing corpses?"

Newt inhaled deeply. Now, Mia had stirred Sabine into a tizzy. There were times the two women fed off each other when it came to overreacting. "Mia, Snookie is safe. I think you should ask your dad about fixing the electric fence because Snookie is an escape artist. And Sabine, I'm not about to arrest anyone. But I do have to ask if anyone knows Kirby Morgan and the last time anyone saw him?"

-4-

Trying to Grow Kentucky Bluegrass in Georgia red clay.

Kirby Morgan?" Sabine echoed. "He's the guy that owned this farm! What's his arm doing here? Where's the rest of him?"

"Sabine, if I knew that, I wouldn't ask the question." Newt explained in an exaggerated patient tone. "Now, Mia, I'm not accusing you or your dog of murder. You're not even a person of interest. All we need to know is if you knew Mr. Morgan or anything you can tell me."

"He knocked on our door one day about three years ago and wanted to see if Daddy would sell him some acreage." Mia began. "Daddy's family owned Summer Flame peach orchard back in the 1900's but after the Great Depression, it went bust. Daddy still held on to the original farm. When Kirby offered to pay three times the appraised value, Daddy leapt on it. He and Momma could pay off the house and retire early. Caleb could attend the Coast Guard Academy and they bought me a car. He even talked about going back to school to finish his degree. You know Daddy always wanted to be a crime scene hobbyist after he watched that episode of CSI a few years ago..."

Newt interrupted, “Look Mia, I don't need to know about all the backstory yet. Just tell me when was the last time you saw him and where."

Mia deliberated for a minute. "About two years ago when he showed at The Store one Monday afternoon and started yelling at Daddy. Kirby said the land was fallow and he couldn't grow any grass or hay or whatever his weird animals ate. He accused Daddy of not disclosing the land was bad. Daddy reminded him that we were in the worst drought in history. Daddy called Kirby a fool for trying grow Kentucky Bluegrass in Georgia red clay. Kirby got mad, shot the finger at Daddy and told him to go to..." Mia tossed her head to search for her mother before she muttered quietly. "He said Daddy should go to ‘effin hell.’ That guy sure did have a temper."

Newt nodded thoughtfully. "Do you know if he was married or had any relatives?"

Mia shrugged her shoulders. "He was married to Marie or Moriah or...was it Maven?"

Sabine could keep silent no longer. "How are you going to find the rest of him?"

"Oh, Snookie can track." Mia hooted excitedly. "Newt, give the bone for Snookie to sniff and we'll see if she can take us to the body."

"Thanks for the offer, Mia. We've called in the K9 officer and his partner from Gwinnett County to nose around."

"What happened to the K9 duo we shared with Hooks County?" Sabine had met the dog's handler, Deputy Sims, several times and he was always very polite and kind.

"Early retirement." Newt dropped his voice to whisper. "He started drinking Blue Nun wine and was wasted everyday by 2:00 p.m."

"Can't you train another deputy while Deputy Sims gets sober?"

"No, it was Tuttle the K9 officer who started drinking. Dang German Shepherd dog outsmarted his handler and started nosing wine bottles off the shelf in the evidence room. Tuttle took to drinking. The sheriff said it would be too expensive to send the dog through rehab and workman's compensation won't cover it."

-5-

His date towered over him in part to the large head of hair.

Sabine hitched a ride with Mia and Snookie in Mia's VW Beetle, affectionately known as Baby, after checking on an embarrassed Drayton.

"Dang it! I didn't get to check inside the geocache." Sabine slapped herself on the forehead. "I guess I have to find another spot to look for one." She stared hopefully at Mia. "You and Lee can come tomorrow or this afternoon. There's one in Winkie Park. You know... your special make out spot with Lee."

"I am not going to bulldoze my way through underbrush just for you. I don't have my septic tank shoes and I have to go back to work." Part of Mia's job was to evaluate the homes of families in need of social services. After going a messy round with sub-par plumbing on her first investigation, Mia switched from her designer pumps to waterproof hiking boots when she met with families. But Sabine knew that wasn't the only reason. According to Mrs. Wallis and despite her denials, Mia was still having nightmares about her last hike in the woods with Sabine, two meth junkies, and the horrible Lindy Mills. "I'm meeting Momma so she can take Snookie home. I hope this doesn't traumatize her."

"Your mom? She's the strongest woman I know."

"No, Snookie. Momma didn't find a skeleton." Mia scoffed at Sabine's inability to follow her train of thought. "Do you want to meet up after work? I can be at The Store at 5:30. We can eat then."

"What? How can you switch topics so fast?" Sabine blew a sweaty lock of hair out of her eyes. "And why do we want to meet up after work?"

"Because we need to make a game plan. If Kirby was murdered, my daddy will be a suspect because of that stupid confrontation at The Store. And when Newt realizes my daddy couldn't hurt a fly, my momma might be up next and then..."

"Your dad threatened to hurt Newt if I ever was mistreated."

Mia pooh-poohed Sabine's concerns. The car whipped into Sabine's driveway. "Please, that's different. That's Southern daddy. Newt will understand that Daddy is harmless. But, he knows Momma isn't a delicate flower and she has a mean streak when she gets riled up. We're lucky I didn't inherit that vindictive gene."

After Mia dropped her off, Sabine hurried to finish the rough draft of the geocaching article as well as an article for the Greenleaf Journal, the county's only newspaper. Although it was only published Saturday night and Wednesday, it was too late for tomorrow, but she would be fired as fast as Dingo devouring her weekly pig ear treat. The publisher, Regina Bethesda, would want to print something besides the new gossip column penned by Chet Chat, an obvious nom de plume of a native. Odds were running two to one that Chet was actually Denise Wallis with Lottie McCall running a very distant second. Hopefully, the newspaper could use the pictures of the Animal Safari she took for the magazine article.

After soaking in the tub for twenty minutes, Sabine toweled herself off and sprayed on Newt's favorite scent—Doggie's Cucumber Mint Deodorant for Smelly Furry Friends. Sabine had accidentally spritzed Dingo's cologne spray when dressing for their first date and Newt had commented on how fresh she smelled. And dang it, she had eventually grown to love it too.

Idly, she logged on the laptop and typed in Kirby Morgan. Not surprisingly, the first few entries were from the Greenleaf Journal archives. One link connected her to the incident where a few juveniles had opened the gates of the safari. The farm had been in business for eight months. Their antics allowed the majority of the animals to roam freely around the county. Kirby was quoted as saying that he believed a local restaurateur was responsible for the crime. Kirby's justification for his suspicion was due to his raising the prices due to feed costs. He even implied that the mystery meat served on Wednesday at this particular diner came from one of his escaped animals.

Even a non-native Greenleafer such as Sabine knew that the restaurateur Kirby was referring to was Paw-Paw Lyons, co-owner of The Store.

Sabine burrowed in her desk for a pen and paper to jot down the information. In that same week in September, Kirby and his date attended the annual Chicken Daze Ball honoring the community's most important industry. Kirby made a significant donation to the festival's operating costs.

"See picture on page 7." Sabine muttered as she pressed enter. While the picture slowly loaded, she eyed Kirby to commit his image to memory. He was a diminutive balding man who looked at ease in his tuxedo. His date towered over him in part to the large head of hair that seemed to have a life of its own.

"Oh no. I just didn't see that." Sabine spoke to Dingo who yawned with great boredom.

"'Local entrepreneur, Kirby Morgan, looking dapper in his custom-tailored tuxedo escorts his current lady, a beaming Charlotte McCall, to celebrate Jaemore County's most profitable business–the poultry processing plants,'" she read out loud. "Oh, this is too good." She quickly printed the articles including the picture. "Kirby's married and he's stepping out with Lotta Hair. I wonder how she reacted when someone told her the marital status of her boyfriend." She jotted that down along with Kirby's wife. After all, any self-respecting wife would be furious if her husband was having an affair with Lottie. Sabine didn't like her but Mia really hated her so this information would make Mia's day.

Lottie McCall and Mia had been at each other throats since first grade when Lottie tried to steal Mia's Twinkie from her Animaniacs lunchbox. As they grew older, the insults and tensions grew. To this day, Sabine still had to mediate between the two if they were in the same room.

A quick glance at her clock told her she needed to finish up her internet search soon. Another newspaper archive showed the new business opening with Kirby and Mayor Crumbee cutting a yellow ribbon with oversize scissors. The article gave scant details but did mention how Kirby and his only full-time employee, Drayton Wilcox, hoped to make the Exotic Animal Safari Atlanta's premier non-traditional meat provider.

"Yes." Sabine punched the air when she remembered Drayton's off the cuff comment about how he told Kirby not to cut down all the peach trees. Should she add Drayton to her list of people that were angry at Kirby Morgan? Yes, if she wanted to clear any of the Wallis family including Snookie, she should add him despite the fact Lee considered him a friend. Kirby's ignorance of proper regional horticulture led Drayton to the unemployment line and a significant career change when the business folded.

Despite Dingo's disinterest, Sabine had managed to uncover three more persons of interest. At least four people had cause to disconnect Kirby's arm from the rest of his body. Paw-Paw Lyons, Drayton

Wilcox, the merry Widow Morgan, and now Mia's arch-nemesis, Lottie aka "Lotta Hair" McCall all had motive. The burning question was where was the rest of Kirby?

-6-

Found herself a man the old-fashioned way

"Mrs. Wallis and Mia are over there." June Bug Lyons, the waitress du jour, pointed into the crowded diner without looking up from her tabloid magazine. "Tonight's dish is chili and cornbread." She informed Sabine as if Sabine didn't know that The Store had a set menu for every day except Saturday and had never deviated from that since the Lyons opened up the restaurant.

"Thanks, June Bug." Sabine offered and refrained from pointing out that true chili does not have beans and at best, The Store's chili should be called a meat and bean stew. But Sabine didn't want to get on June Bug's bad side again. She had set her sights on Newt earlier in the year despite Newt's polite refusal. As a result, Sabine couldn't eat at The Store for a month or so after she and Newt started dating. She didn't want to find any stray cigarette butts or strange fauna in her chili as a retaliation.

In a move to allow Sabine back to The Store, Mia helped June Bug build a dating profile on a popular website but to everyone's shock, she found herself a man the old fashioned way—meeting newly paroled prisoners. Melvin Johnson had been released for good behavior and was visiting his late cousin's wife, Nancy, in the Lyons family compound. Nancy was June Bug's older sister. Romance blossomed over Melvin's appreciation for June Bug's tattoos as Melvin apparently a master tattoo artist.

Sabine slid into the plastic booth across from Mia and her mom. Mrs. Wallis, just as beautiful as her daughter, considered Sabine as one of her own children.

"I went ahead and ordered for you." Mrs. Wallis smiled.

"Here." June Bug's son, Dickie, interrupted the conversation and thrust the basket of cornbread on the table. His right arm filled with three large bowls of chili.

Mrs. Wallis arched an eyebrow. "Dickie Johnson, there's no reason to be rude. It wasn't our fault you got fired from the Cliff's 7/11 store and have to work here. You should have not posted on Facebook and identified people who buy contraceptives from a convenience store."

Dickie looked chastised. "Sorry, Miz Wallis. I didn't mean to take it out on y'all." He turned on his heel and fled back into the kitchen.

Sabine snagged a piece of hot cornbread and slathered it with butter while Mia and Mrs. Wallis studied the Journal printouts.

"Oh, baby girl, you have done great!" Mrs. Wallis grinned. "This should keep us busy for a few days while Newt is searching for Kirby. And maybe this will convince Micah that he is not the prime suspect. I swear your father was so thrilled to be considered as the bad guy. That's what I get for letting him enroll in that online crime scene technician program from Jamaica and buy that blue light on EBay."

Mia was equally happy. "At least he stopped using all the cornstarch as fingerprint powder. And Lotta Hair is a suspect! That, Sabine, is the best news. And look at that dress she wore to the ball. Anyone with a smidgeon of fashion sense could have told her that gown was last year's knockoff of a Chanel runway outfit."

After a few moments of inhaling the spicy chili, Mrs. Wallis daintily wiped her mouth.

"Let's talk strategy. I'll handle Lottie since both of my kids can't manage to be civil to her. Mia, stop." Mrs. Wallis held up her hand. "I can't trust you not to plant some sort of evidence to frame her. Lord knows she deserves it but now is not the time for petty differences."

"You can plant anything in that hair and you'd never find it even if you had a back-ho." Mia muttered as Sabine took a sip of sweet tea to disguise her laughter.

"Mia, you take Paw-Paw and try to see if any one of the Lyons would do it. You know what I mean—

some of those Lyons like that ten-year-old Elvis Lyons could probably take down Homeland Security but feel them out to see if anyone had opportunity. Remember your dad's freedom is at stake so no mercy." She shuffled the papers.

"And Mavis Augustine Morgan. I know she was in a sorority at Auburn University." Both Wallis women frowned at the mention of another arch-rival of the nearby University of Georgia. Both ladies were proud graduates and considered any other institute of higher learning inferior although they did make an exception for Sabine's alma mater, Texas A&M even though the Aggies were a Southeastern Conference West school. Sabine did not look forward to the day when her beloved Texas Ags meet the Bulldogs on the gridiron. She had a feeling that no one was going to be happy the next day.

"I'm surprised that Kirby and Mavis married. Rumor had it that a distant relative of Kirby's actually sold lumber to a Yankee during Reconstruction and Mavis' family had roots in Atlanta when it was called Terminus. Maybe love conquered all."

"If we don't find anything on those suspects, we'll move on to Drayton Wilcox. I had forgotten that Drayton worked for Kirby. He wasn't with that job long but there may be some more history we can get from him. We'll have to ask Lee how to approach that."

"I can talk to Drayton." Sabine offered and then crossed her eyes as a stray thought tried to coalesce in her brain. Mia noticed this and elbowed her mother.

"Momma, Sabine's making that weird face again like she's trying to think of something but nothing is coming out. Should we talk her down?"

At that moment, cells phones chirped or rang simultaneously. Faster than Jesse James, Mia whipped out her phone.

"They found the rest of Kirby under a tree. Let's roll."

Sabine hijacked the last piece of cornbread and grabbed her sweet tea as Mrs. Wallis threw down some cash and joined the departing herd of rubberneckers streaming out The Store.

-7-

Yep, that's a skeleton. The person is probably dead.

Sabine recognized Tucker Johnson's faded blue 1974 Impala at the front of the strange procession to view what everyone assumed to be Kirby Morgan's remains. Tucker's car trunk was still tied down with twine after park rangers opened it forcefully during a drug bust. Excitement was slim pickings in Jaemore County and any upheaval, no matter how ghoulish or insane, held an atmosphere of excitement or even gaiety for the citizens.

"Oh, Momma! Look two cars behind us. It's Ms. Tilda's Caddy! Do you think the old bat has come out of seclusion?" Mia bubbled like a five-year-old at Christmas. "And maybe Lotta Hair is with her!"

Matilda Greenleaf Jaemore was the grand dame of high society in the area. The Greenleaf family, aided by the Jaemores. settled the area in 1803. Her only grandson and sole successor to the family money, Mick Jaemore, dated Lindy Mills. Lindy was the mastermind of the encroaching meth problem into the county. Mick also fathered an adorable daughter with Arial Bixby. Both Mick and Arial were alcoholics but were going through treatment. Lindy tried to kill not only Arial but Sabine and Mia last spring. Ms. Tilda had retreated into the Jaemore Manor and had not been seen in since.

"Oh, this would be exciting." Mrs. Wallis' eyes gleamed. "It would make sense. This murder replaces Mick's alcohol problem and his baby Kayla as the latest gossip, not that I would know about spreading bad gossip." Mia immediately wanted to make it a statement of fact she did not participate in gossip before her mother could admonish her. She knew her mother could spout scripture on the sins of the tongue and breaking the commandment of bearing false witness.

Sabine pointed to the dilapidated entrance where the geocache was. "There's that horrid reporter, Sally Jackson from Channel 7 news doing a live update. It figures she'd be out here. I didn't think she could go outside while the sun was up." Sabine sniggered and crossed herself. Sally Jackson had covered or over dramatized the death of Louis Dixon and Lindy Mill's methamphetamine operation. There was a not-so-subtle hatred between Sally and Jaemore County or 'the Armpit of Georgia' as the erstwhile reporter labeled the county.

Mrs. Wallis tooted her horn to wave at Sally. That prompted the rest of the rubberneckers to honk ruining Sally's live report. One person managed to toss a full cup of sweet tea on Sally and her cameraman. Sabine normally hated to witness such a blatant waste of the "champagne of the South" but in this case, Sabine berated herself for not thinking of it first.

When Tucker's Impala took a right onto a gravel road a few hundred yards before the entrance to Summerflame Trail subdivision, the procession moved at the pace of a sloth.

Sabine nodded in approval. "This makes sense. Your subdivision borders the animal farm. And y'all's house backs right up to the boundary. Snookie probably didn't go as far as we thought to dig up Kirby."

Mrs. Wallis beeped at her husband who was lounging under a tall oak reading a vintage Sports Illustrated Swimsuit edition when they passed the Wallis' backyard. A cacophony of honking followed them when each car paraded past Micah Wallis who resembled a beauty pageant winner waving at his admirers.

"This is where the farm's supplies were dropped off." Mia recalled the steady flow of delivery trucks. "For the first three months, it was a constant stream of trucks. Do you remember, Momma?"

Mrs. Wallis nodded in agreement. "If you recall, one of those truckers lost control and barreled through Mrs. Hughes privacy fence and her prized hydrangea bushes."

"Boy was she mad!" Mia giggled. "Especially when she tried to accuse Daddy of orchestrating it."

The Wallis' long-time next-door neighbor, Mrs. Hughes, or 'Old Lady Hughes' as she was not affectionately known, had always disliked the Wallises. From the daily "Taps" blaring while Mr. Wallis raised the US flag and the KIA/MIA flag, to a regrettable incident between Old Lady Hughes' unkempt poodle, Andre, and an in-heat Snookie, the two houses seemed like an armed camp poised for war.

A mile later Mrs. Wallis skillfully parked her BMW on the side of the road near a large field of kudzu behind the Impala as all the other cars followed suit. "Remember where we parked!"

Sabine seized her tote bag containing all of what a rural Lois Lane would need. "I'll need to get pictures for the Journal and maybe a quote from the sheriff."

"Already ahead of you." Mia executed a perfect jump before the car stopped moving and shoved her way to the front of the crowd. "I'll see if I can snag something from Newt or Tim-Tom the Obtuse Coroner."

Sabine and Mrs. Wallis gently elbowed their way through the burgeoning crowd. Sabine could just see the top of the tree where everyone had gathered. One enterprising Lyons boy was even selling cold soft drinks giving the throng an almost carnival vibe.

"Hey, no skipping ahead." An angry, bald man with a pronounced lip ring and large heart tattoo on his neck growled.

"Sabine." Mrs. Wallis fanned herself quickly. "Help this poor senior citizen to her daughter. And you, Melvin Thompson, need to learn some manners. After all, you just got sprung from that prison in South Georgia. Do you want to go back? Because I can make that happen!"

Melvin's face reflected disappointment and his heart tattoo drooped. "Sorry Miz Wallis. I didn't mean nothing by it. It's just nice to be on the other side of the police tape instead of being cuffed."

"Now whose fault is that? No one told you to rob that fast food joint with a tattoo needle. You only got away with $45. Granny Lureen always said, 'If you're going to do a job, give it your all.'"

"Mrs. Wallis, we need to find Mia. Remember our discussion back at The Store?" Sabine interrupted.

"Thank you, hon. I'll see you later Melvin." Mrs. Wallis' voice softened and lowered. "I know you're still looking for a job. If you still need some work, come by my office this Saturday. I'll have some things that need to be done around the building before we do our tailgating at the Georgia-Vanderbilt game. If you do a good job, I know Maxi Masters from Handy Girl is looking for an assistant and I'll recommend you."

Melvin gushed. "Oh, thanks Miz Wallis. I'll be there at 9 at your office!"

Sabine's eyes darted over to her Georgia mother. "I got your number."

"What fool thing are you talking about, hon?" Mrs. Wallis searched the crowd for Mia.

"You're a big gummy bear inside, aren't you? You act all big and bad and then you go and do something nice like helping someone. Mia told me that you're helping Arial Bixby with her real estate license and still paying her as your receptionist even though she goes with you during showings. And you helped Shay Edmunds, Tim-Tom's ex-wife, find a good daycare provider after the divorce was final."

Mrs. Wallis looked embarrassed. "Sshhh. Don't go spreading that around. I have a reputation to protect. Anyway, both Shay and Arial needed a break and my Granny Lureen always preached that if you can lend a hand then you can surely lend your wallet, too."

"She was the same one who said, 'If you gotta put down roots, come to me for fertilizing,' wasn't she?"

"What took you so long?" Mia hissed. "I managed to snag a picture of our idiot coroner, Tim-Tom, talking to Newt. And I got a quote. Tim-Tom said, 'Yep, that's a skeleton. The person is probably dead.' And I managed to chip a nail." She held out her slender hand and pointed to a minute speck on her left index finger.

"I'm not using that as a quote. 'Probably dead' describes Tim-Tom Edmunds' brain activity." Sabine scoffed at the witless coroner. Coroners in the state of Georgia did not need degrees or apparently, in Jaemore County's case, a functioning brain. They only needed to complete a certification offered by some sort of police academy. It was one of the last holdouts of the good old boy system. "What else can we get?"

"What about a diversion?" Mia piped up energetically. "Momma, can you pretend to faint? No. No one would believe that. Sabine, fall down and grab your ankle. You're so klutzy everyone would believe it. Oh, there's an old ant mound. Pretend you're stung and scream to high heaven."

"I'm not that klutzy." Sabine scowled. "And it's too late in the season for ants. Anyway, you had the broken ankle not me. You also made a big profit from that break."

During the explosion of the meth lab from last spring, Mia had suffered a hairline fracture in her ankle. While she was aggrieved to have her leather boots cut to treat the injury, Mia made her cane covers to hide the unsightly gray metal of the cane. Thinking ahead, she designed to be interchangeable and match the fashionable klutz's daily outfit. She made more than a few dollars during that enterprise.

"OH MY GOD! A SNAKE WITH A RAT!!" Melvin Thompson's voice rose several octaves higher than a ten-year-old girl. "Coming out of the kudzu!" With that, the hardened criminal swooned faster than Melanie Wilkes in *Gone with the Wind* and fell to the ground.

That started another stampede of Greenleafers, this time over the police tape and trampling the crime scene near a large peach tree while Newt glowered, knowing anything he could do would be ineffective.

Sabine ducked under dodging hysterical citizens and eased up under the old tree where the tarp lay. Using her pen, she lifted it up and without fanfare or focusing, snapped picture after picture on her cell phone. She eased back and merged with the crowd. Everyone seemed to wait to see what Newt would do with the reptile. She sidled up with her boyfriend. "Aren't you going shoot it?"

"No. That snake has every reason to be in the kudzu. And I should be confiscating your phone by the way." Newt's voice was mild as he observed the snake slither back into the kudzu, unaware of the chaos it caused.

"What? Why? How?" Sabine rushed out. "I don't..."

"You know exactly. If I didn't know better, I would think that you trained that snake." Newt pivoted back to the crowd. "Everyone needs to leave. You're trampling a crime scene." He glowered at his girlfriend as most of the horde retreated.,

Sabine look affronted while she covertly saved the pictures to her Cloud account. "You know I don't like snakes. Here. If it will improve your disposition, I'll delete the pictures I took." She made a great show of pulling up the pictures and deleting each one.

Newt closed his hand over her phone. "I'm teasing. This is not the real crime scene. I staged it because I knew exactly something like this would happen once the call hit the scanners. All you did was take pictures of a few rocks and litter." He motioned toward a large oak fifty yards to the east that was ringed with yellow tape. His voice dropped. "But to make up for it, if you want, I'll give you a quote." He leaned in making their foreheads touch. "Maybe tonight. I'll have to frisk you."

Sabine's heart immediately jumped into overdrive and a flush colored her face. Even after all this time, she still got embarrassed when Newt talked like that.

"Newton G. Johansson. I don't know what you're talking about but it clearly is not for polite company." Mrs. Wallis' voice carried over the melee. "Sabine Anne, get yourself over here and help me back to the car. I have an appointment to show a house and it's obvious you can't be unchaperoned." The heat was getting to Mrs. Wallis. A thin film of sweat gleamed across her forehead.

After settling back into the leather seats of the BMW, Sabine scrolled through but stopped when she spied Mrs. Wallis' hands tighten over the steering wheel. Her lower lip was non-existent and held in place between her teeth. Rarely, did she bite her bottom lip and when she did it was not a good sign.

"What's wrong?" Sabine was truly concerned. Mrs. Wallis never showed any type of anxiety.

Mrs. Wallis heaved a heavy sigh. "That's the Summer Flame peach tree where Micah proposed to me. And now to think that Kirby Morgan has been rotting under it makes my stomach turn."

Mia paused filing her nails and injected, "That wasn't the crime scene, Momma. I flirted with Tim-Tom a bit. The real grave was in the kudzu."

"That's what you get for flirting with an idiot." Sabine scrunched her nose at Mia. "Newt said it was the big oak tree fifty yards away."

"Well..." Mia searched for an appropriate comeback. "At least, I confirmed someone died. And...and your hair is frizzing."

"Ppffft," Sabine blew an errant strand of red hair from her eyes. "Just admit it. I got the better 4-1-1."

Mrs. Wallis raised her right hand. "Just stop it. Sisters should not be bickering like y'all do."

"But Momma, we're not sisters." Mia corrected. "She's weird and her imaginary voices won't even talk to her. She's white and I'm black. And you're black. We were all black until the little Miss Redhead Psychotic Orphan from Texas showed up a year..."

"Mia!" Mrs. Wallis interrupted her sharply. "Love doesn't care about color or blood or where you're from." Mrs. Wallis' eyes shone bright with tears.

Sabine also felt the telltale burning in her eyes and was touched at the declaration of love. "Thanks, Mrs. Wallis."

"Just accept the fact that Sabine outdid you this time with info gathering, Mia." Mrs. Wallis turned to smile at Sabine. "My little baby is all growing up and getting all the good gossip scoops. Not that I approve of gossiping. It's not gossip until you tell someone else."

-8-

I'm open to any sort of electro-shock therapy or medication

Sabine stood in front of her bathroom mirror the next morning and mentally practiced her side of the phone call to Mavis. She had researched Mavis Morgan, only to discover Kirby Morgan's former wife lived in an exclusive community on Tuxedo Road in Buckhead, one of Atlanta's most affluent neighborhoods. Mavis was a big contributor to the Atlanta Symphony Orchestra and a docent at the Higgens Museum of Modern Art. She also was a noted supporter of the Singa-Sphynx Cat Rescue of the Deep South.

"May I please speak to Mavis Augustine Morgan? Is this Mavis? Is Ms. Morgan available?" Nope, the Texas drawl permeated and defeated Sabine's attempt to sound snooty. If Mavis had a brain and according to Mia, it was doubtful since she went to Auburn, Sabine wouldn't get past the front gate.

A loud burp emanated from the bedroom. Sabine frowned and then shuddered when the smell hit. Dingo had the smelliest body emissions. Even changing her dog food didn't curb the noxious odors. The elderly vet out of Greenleaf, Dr. Emberly, had just shrugged his shoulders and informed Sabine to watch Dingo's diet. Then a light bulb popped. Time to get Dingo to the doctor.

A few minutes later after checking out the Singa-Sphynx Cat Rescue page and the link to the charity's preferred veterinary clinic, Sabine had her way in. According to the site, Dr. Mitchell Lana was a proud alumnus of the Universidade Integradas Plinio Leite in Brazil and now a partner in the prestigious Tuxedo Animal Clinic in Buckhead. He was a big believer in "living one with nature and letting the animal chart its own course." Sabine crinkled her nose. Once he smelled Dingo, he'd see the cleaner side of living with air freshener and showing the Aussie the nearest road out of town.

"Yes, I'd like to make an appointment with Dr. Lana. My Australian Shepherd is having digestive problems." Sabine watched Dingo lick her stubby tail and her hairy bottom. To further assert her dominance, Dingo began to pant onto Sabine's pillow. "She also has some behavior problems. Could I make an appointment with the doctor as soon as possible? I've heard he's the best in the state dealing with problem animals."

Dingo shot Sabine a dirty look as if she understood everything her owner said. Without taking her eyes off her, Dingo snatched Sabine's pillow and flung it off the bed.

"And I'm open to any sort of electro-shock therapy or medication to correct the behavior." Sabine glared at her dog. Dingo clawed her way under the blanket on Sabine's side. "Oh, you don't do that type of therapy. Well...whatever it takes...she can have an extended stay with y'all. Tomorrow at 11 is fine. And she might need her yearly immunizations – you know the ones with the big needles. Thank you." Sabine pressed the end button and turned toward Dingo. "Who's the alpha now? Huh? Now get off my blanket."

"I know Dingo does not need any immunizations. I took her to Dr. Emberly myself at the beginning of summer." Newt called from the doorway. "What are you up to?" He wrangled his tie on and shrugged on his coat. Court had been temporarily suspended because of the discovery of the skeletal remains. But Newt was due for another long day, this time being cross examined by local defense attorney Hamilton Bilbo, Jaemore County's version of pond scum.

Sabine strolled nonchalantly toward him while attempted a sexy smile. "It's an exam. I'm worried about her burping. But that's enough about the dog. Didn't you say you were going to frisk me? You got home too late last night, and you were exhausted."

"Not now. Can't you see Dingo is clearly upset? You probably threw her off the bed and now look at her. She is burrowing her nose in your shoe. All she wants is your love." Newt bent over and scratched the Aussie. "I'm not sure when I'll be home. After court, I have to go downtown to the GBI Crime Lab so I'll be late tonight."

Sabine nodded absently. "What?"

Newt straightened his tie in the mirror. "You know, the Georgia Bureau of Investigation? The state cops? That's where the skeleton is since Jaemore County doesn't have facilities for an autopsy."

Newt shoved his wallet in his pocket. "There is a package waiting for me from Sweden at the post office. Mor just airmailed me the ingredients for *surströmming*."

During the past six months, Newt and Sabine traded off cooking supper, slowly introducing their own take on food to each other. Sabine favored the slow grilling and spicy food of her Texas home while Newt labored hard to instill a love of Swedish cuisine partly due to his mother, or 'Mor,' as he called her. For the most part, Sabine was able to acquire a taste of food that required Google translator to pronounce, but *surströmming,* or fermented herring, tested the limits of her palate. Even Dingo, who was the canine equivalent to a turkey vulture, couldn't stomach the fish.

Newt didn't notice Sabine's grimace and continued. "Mor and Far want to fly in for Thanksgiving if you're okay with that. They've never had a proper Thanksgiving meal." He glanced and finally saw Sabine's look of alarm. "It's okay. They are going to stay in my apartment. There's no pressure. You're a big part of my life and I want them to meet you."

In two giant steps, he reached Sabine and enveloped her in a hug. "They don't have to come. I can fly to Sweden in November."

"Newt." Sabine's voice was muffled in his chest. "It's not your parents visiting. They're more than welcome. You know we're going to Texas at Christmas so you'll meet everyone at the Metzke Insane Asylum. It's just that I can't stomach any *surströmming*."

"Oh! I'm glad because I want to talk to you about Thanksgiving. Why don't you get takeout The Store and after I get home, we'll eat. Later on, I'll finish frisking you?"

"Now that's an awesome idea. I've got to meet up with Drayton at Winkie Park for the geocaching article follow-up in a few hours." Sabine shooed Dingo away from her shoes and slid her right foot into a mush of something wet, gooey and full of twigs. "Dingo! You little butthead. Get over here. You barfed in my shoe!"

-9-

The scariest part of Jaemore County was the citizens.

"Drayton, you said yesterday that you worked for Kirby Morgan." Sabine darted a glance at her companion as they navigated a heavily wooded area of Winkie Park. She didn't dare keep her eyes off the brush, having read up on copperheads and other venomous, not poisonous, snakes. Winkie Park was also allegedly the home of a humongous boa constrictor named Julius Squeezer, Greenleaf's most popular urban legend. There were also legends of a lost Chupacabra that came over during the Bay of Pigs in the early sixties. Sabine and Mia hypothesized that the scariest part of Jaemore County was the citizens. Sabine didn't want to run into anything remotely dangerous or skeletal.

Drayton removed his hat and gazed in the direction of an empty playground. "Yeah. Nice guy but he was stubborn. Thought he knew everything about the restaurant business. He may have, but he didn't know squat about Georgia weather and farming."

"What happened?" Sabine had grabbed a stick and was poking path through the brambles and brush.

"He cared more about the appearance of the farm at first. He wanted to impress clients so he plowed up all the old peach trees and planted St. Augustine grass because Bermuda grass wasn't pretty enough. St. Augustine grass doesn't grow north of Macon and can't function in full sun during a drought. In the end, he couldn't sustain the business because the bison needed the grass that couldn't grow because of the drought so he had to import feed. There was some bad blood between him and a chef in Atlanta that got pretty heated. Then Kirby expended more cash to start a petting zoo but only was able to buy a few animals. The final nail in the coffin was when someone or some kids released the bison, donkeys, anteaters, ostriches and camels. Some he got back and some were probably hunted down and eaten. This is, after all, still a rural area. He never recovered after that."

Sabine kicked a log to look under it for the geocache, motioning for Drayton to poke at the leaves beside it. "Did the police investigate when Kirby disappeared?"

Drayton shook his head. "No, that's the weird thing. No one knew he disappeared. He went to a fundraiser for some chicken festival and the following morning, he went to The Store to fuss at Paw-Paw Lyons and saw Micah Wallis. They got into it and we all thought Kirby left to go back to his wife in Atlanta when he didn't show up at the farm the next day."

Sabine detected a note of uncertainty in Drayton's voice. "But you didn't think so?"

"No." Drayton heaved a big sigh. "Kirby had found the remains of a basement near the stone chimney. When he discovered that it was the old Wallis cabin built in the 1870's after the Civil War, he worked his tail off to restore it. He read up on local history and even donated to the Historical Society. Because money was getting tight, he put a lot of sweat equity into it. He learned woodworking, carpentry, and rudimentary electrical skills. Kirby even read up on historic stone masonry to restore the chimney to its former use since chimneys were the heart of the cabins. He changed for the better. He started caring more about the land when he worked it. Oh, he still had a temper, but his outlook went from all business to thinking maybe a legacy is not just being rich and powerful. He was so stinking proud of the fact he restored that chimney just like it had been in the 19th century. He even showed it off to Lottie."

Drayton sighed again but sniffed as if he was tearing up. "After the chimney was restored, he turned his attention to the basement. There were several large nests of bees Kirby found when excavating the basement. They had burrowed into the old wood support beams. Kirby was highly allergic to bees so he had to hire the exterminator.

This was the last day I saw Kirby. We had went over into Gwinnett County to study period architecture. But he was a no show the next day and the pest girl sent the bill into Kirby's Atlanta office. Kirby was such a meticulous businessman and would never have let a contractor show up and he pay the bill without knowing if the contractor actually did the job. It just doesn't gee haw.

"When I raised a red flag, the Sheriff's Office called his office in Atlanta and claimed they investigated but found nothing so nothing was ever done about a disappearance. I should have known calling Sheriff Ostermeyer was a waste of time. This was before your boyfriend came on board." Drayton hung his head. "I should have followed up. It's my fault. I let Ostie handle it, knowing he's a joke."

Sabine heaved a sigh when another search of leaves around a tree for the geocache came up empty. "Well, it's not your fault, Drayton. Everyone knows the sheriff's office was a joke until Newt came along. And as to the circumstances around his disappearance, I can't really say. I didn't meet Kirby so I don't know why he would react that way. But yeah, it sounds kind of hinky. Newt told me over dinner last night that the dental records positively identified it as Kirby. Sadly, there was no exact cause of death. You don't know if he fell, had a heart attack or was even murdered."

Drayton didn't seem comforted by Sabine's assertion. "Kirby was a nice guy but he was a businessman first. When he got a bee in his bonnet, if you pardon the analogy since he was allergic to bees, he didn't let up until he was satisfied. He made a few enemies here, not deadly enemies, just people who didn't like him. One being Paw-Paw because the Lyons refused to buy any exotic animals for their menu. Then I heard him saying he had to get a restraining order against some wacko animal group who opposed raising animals for food. And then there was Mr. Wallis. Mr. Wallis refused to sell that land until Kirby offered a pretty penny for it and Kirby screwed up the land by all that clear cutting. But anyone who knows this area knows it's not Mr. Wallis you need to be afraid of–it's Mrs. Wallis." Drayton wiped his forehead.

"And then there was Charlotte McCall. I heard that she was going on about how she landed a millionaire and planned to leave this podunk town. But the thing was, I thought she was truly in love with him. She used to come out and cook lunch for him in his work trailer. Everyone knew Kirby and Mavis were not a love match in the first place. It was purely a business arrangement. Mavis knew the right people and Kirby had the money. I know Lottie is not a looker but Kirby was very fond of her. He was always giving her little gifts. He made her a music box to test his woodworking skills. Very rough looking but still sweet."

Drayton stood up and held out his hand to Sabine. "Let's go find this geocache. I'll buy you a slushy at the 7-11 when we're done."

Sabine brushed more debris around her. "Ick! What is that?" She pointed at Drayton's feet.

"It's...a...dead...squi...." Drayton collapsed in heap beside the newly departed squirrel covered in slime.

-10-

Scaring poor church people and probably invoking the devil.

Sabine dangled a hot dog in front of Dingo to entice her into the Dodge. "Come on. You know I was joking about the shots and the tests. I would not let you get shots again and you know it. Just play nice with this doctor and I'll let you sit between me and Newt tonight." Sabine broke the hot dog into three pieces. "Look, three treats now." Sabine placed one a few feet in front and the other two leading to the open car door.

Dingo yawned. The damn dog was too smart for her own good.

"Fine. We'll stop at Sonic."

At the mention of her favorite restaurant, Dingo inhaled the three treats and raced into the car.

"Finally." Sabine slammed the passenger door and had to push the Aussie out of the driver's seat. Dingo reclined into the canine seat belt restraint. "Just so you know, you're not driving at any time. We're going into Atlanta and you get road rage too easily to be trusted. And I'm leaving off the egg from the Breakfast Toaster from Sonic. I can't handle egg butt tonight."

As usual, Atlanta traffic, even in the late morning, was agonizing. Sabine had learned to drive on the Houston 610 loop but Spaghetti Junction where I-85 and the 285 perimeter met tested even the limits of her skill. Dingo was having none of it. She managed to press the window button to open her side and barked viciously at a church van filled with senior citizens having the audacity to drive the speed limit. One elderly woman on the bus paled alarmingly and pointed at Dingo. Sabine hoped she would not be financially liable for the stroke the woman was sure to have. She hoped the cameras from the HOV lane wouldn't snap a picture of her license plates.

"Stop it. I don't know what you're saying but I'm sure it's full of Aussie profanity. You're scaring poor church people and probably are invoking the devil. I'm locking the windows since you can't control yourself. Thank God you've not figured out how to outmaneuver the seat belt."

Parking was difficult in Buckhead, but Sabine managed to squeeze the Challenger between a yellow Prius with a blue racing stripe and a Vespa. A small red Volkswagen Beetle rounded out the parking lot. A cozy Victorian mansion housed the animal clinic.

A privacy fence wrapped around most of the yard. Even in the car, Sabine could hear a cacophony of animal noises ranging from ducks to pigs to a few unfamiliar sounds.

She turned to her dog with leash in hand and was not surprised to find Dingo had unlocked her seat belt. "How'd you...what kind...?" Sabine stuttered.

Dingo stared pointedly at the leash in hand as if trying to get her owner in gear and get the job over.

"Now, remember, behave. No chasing other pets. No sitting on them. Nothing." Sabine opened the door and welcomed the cool air which was a pleasant change from the humidity and heat.

A striking Indian lady in her early thirties in a colorful ensemble beckoned Sabine and Dingo over to her desk.

"How y'all doin'?" The receptionist grinned, flashing blindingly white teeth.

"Uh..." Sabine and Dingo looked at each and back to the lady.

"Didn't expect a drawl, did ya? I'm Dhwani but you can call me Dee." She stood up and held out her hand.

Dingo sat down and held her paw out as if a queen and shook Dee's hand.

"Oh, what a beautiful sweetheart you are!" Dee gushed and massaged Dingo's ears. Dingo, for her part, gazed lovingly up at her new best friend.

Sabine remembered her manners and smiled just in time to finish the greeting.

"I'm sorry. I wasn't expecting such a..." Sabine searched for the correct word.

"That's okay, darlin'. You didn't expect a Southern belle to greet you. I get it all the time. I was born just outside Ahmedabad, you know on the west coast of India but my daddy, bless his heart, wanted his girls—I'm the fifth out of seven—to have a freedom his momma didn't have so we moved here when I was almost five. I'm a Georgia peach through and through. My late momma taught me how to cook traditional Hindi food with a Georgia twist. That's my hobby, you know. Fusion baking. Here—have some *sohan halwa* with pecans and apple pie dip." Dee motioned to a delectable ensemble of cookies. She hooked her arm around Sabine's and led her to the desk brushing off Dingo's hair from her clothing.

When Dee saw Sabine's pained expression at the clinging fur, she shooed her hand at Dingo. "Don't you worry your pretty little head about my shalwar kameez. This old outfit has seen worse things than a few tufts of dog hair." Dee leaned in further and winked. "I actually wear this to hide my tushie. One too many desserts at the Blue Willow Inn over in Social Circle. And too many taste tests for my orange chiffon cake topped with homemade *kulfi*."

Sabine's head spun trying to reconcile all the information. Dee continued to chatter while she took Dingo back to weigh her. Sabine bit into one of Dee's cookies topped with an apple glaze and almost cried out in pleasure. She stuffed the rest of the cookie in her mouth and plucked a brochure about the animal practice and its two locations serving the wealthy elite. It also publicized that Dr. Lana was bilingual in Spanish and English. When they returned, Dingo was crunching on a treat and Dee picked up where she left off in their conversation.

"I've been working here as a vet assistant since I was sixteen and then got promoted to office manager a few years later after I finished my bachelor's degree. That's been fifteen years ago. Wow and I have to say, your Dingo is just about the most well-behaved dog. She has the most beautiful markings."

"She does." Sabine agreed but privately thought it was fortunate that Dingo was unique and stood out in a crowd. Blue merle and marbled eyes made for an easy wanted poster for the police. "Fifteen years. And this is such a great location. I bet you get a lot of frou-frou dogs and cats."

Dee nodded. "We sure do. The other day one of the high society ladies brought in a Mal-Shi. That's a cross between a Maltese and Shih Tzu. Furry little yapping dog who bit anyone who went too close. I told Dr. Lana that maybe it needed a warm enema and some Xanax to calm down. He didn't agree or appreciate my suggestion." Dee frowned briefly at the mention of Dr. Lana. "After all this time, I never thought I would dislike a vet. Why, there are times I think I know more about veterinary medicine than he does. Why, he usually only does well checkups and sends..."

Dee stopped in midsentence as she just remembered where she was. "Anyway, I work here because I love animals. When Momma died a few years ago, she left all her girls a good sum of money she had invested in a little old pharmaceutical company when it was just started out and pretty soon, Momma was a multimillionaire. When she died, her money was divided up among her girls. I just let it sit there." Dee chuckled. "Why, I don't even know how much I have in my account."

"I think it's awesome you work here because you help animals." Sabine was impressed. If Dee was telling the truth, the office manager was the most unpretentious millionaire in history. "Speaking of rich people..." Sabine kicked herself for such an obvious segue way. "Do you know..." Sabine tapped her chin as in deep thought. "Does Mavis Morgan bring in her pets here? I met her at a party a few months ago and I think she lives not too far away." Sabine smiled benignly.

"You mean Mavis Augustine? She and Dr. Lana are like two peas in a pod. They started that weird cat rescue—Singalong or something like that." Dee tilted her head and shook her finger. "But, Sabine, if you were acquaintances, you'd know she never used Morgan even though they married years ago. She's too proud of her family name. She's a descendant of General Marcellus Stovall's best friend from West Point. He—Stovall, not the friend—was a Confederate general. Her ancestor was a blockade runner or pirate depending on who you ask out of Savannah. And as you know, for some, it's all about your people down here."

Sabine's shoulders drooped. She truly sucked at lying. "Sorry about coming in here with a hidden agenda. The police think her husband, Kirby Morgan, was found. Or rather, his remains were found."

Dee guffawed. "I know. It's all in the news. They positively identified Kirby Morgan from dental records according to Channel 7's 'Daybreak Atlanta' morning show. Sally Jackson has been making daily reports from everywhere in Jaemore County and outside the mansion. And, I might add, in the most hideous outfits. What are you fishin' for?

"My best friend's parents are potential suspects in Kirby's disappearance and a couple of other people I know somehow involved. Nothing's set in stone because they're waiting on a cause of death. I wanted to scout out anybody who might wanted to hurt or even kill him."

Dee dropped her voice to a whisper. "I wouldn't put anything past Madame Augustine. She is a real condescending bee-hotch. You know the kind that gets her feathers ruffled if you don't brown nose enough. Come see me after the visit with Dr. 'Wonderful.'" Dee halted her diatribe and glanced at the time. "Well, look at the time. Follow me with Dingo and Dr. Lana will be with you in a minute."

-11-

Picture a Dallas Cowboy Cheerleader's head on a corpse with a spray tan.

Sabine fidgeted impatiently while Dingo took the opportunity to investigate every sniff able surface. Dr. Lana was a no-show after ten minutes so Sabine pulled up the Singa-Sphynx Cat Rescue to familiarize herself. She didn't want to make a mistake with her story like she did with Dee.

The door flung open and Sabine had scant time to notice Dr. Lana's features. He was relatively young to be in charge of such an affluent practice. Long, dark wavy hair framed his face. The brief smile didn't reach his gray eyes and his nose, obviously broken several times, hung over his lips like a beak. Sabine spied a vortex tattoo on his wrist. He was attractive in a hippie sort of way. He rifled through the information while he made his introduction.

"I'm Dr. Lana."

Sabine thrust out her hand but he was too busy looking at the new client paperwork. Dingo had retreated in front Sabine and tensed while she sat. The fur along her spine raised threateningly and her lip curled up. Clearly, Dr. Lana was on the same level as those emotional terrorist squirrels who lived like squatters in Dingo's backyard.

"Your Aussie has digestive problems. What do you feed her?" He barked out in an abrasive tone. He had no clue that he was about to become part of Dingo's nutritional pyramid.

"Dog food. Sometimes a pig ear. If she finds a crumb on the floor, it's hers." Sabine replied, unsure of what he wanted to hear. She wound the leash a couple of times around her hand when Dingo stood up.

"Unacceptable." He snapped the folder shut and spun on his heel to leave. "Animals know what kind of food they need. You should let her choose what she wants. If you still insist on this master mentality, the practice sells my specially formulated food for animals."

"Uh, shouldn't you, I don't know, examine her or do any tests?"

"Who is the doctor here?"

"But if she chooses, she'll be eating everything in sight including my dinner!"

"Again, who is the doctor here?"

"I..."

Dr. Lana pinched the bridge of his nose with his right hand as if he was preventing an aneurysm. "Look, *Puta.* I have studied this extensively. We humans are imposing our value and thought system on other beings because we won the genetic lottery by developing thumbs. Let. The. Animal. Choose." With that patronizing command, Dr. Lana twirled his white coat like a bad impersonator of Dracula and departed the room.

Sabine glared at the door and then dropped her gaze to Dingo who relaxed her protective stance. "Did that just happen? He cussed at me in Spanish." As a native Houstonian whose German family settled in the area, Sabine knew all the swear words in many languages including Spanish and German with a Korean phrase learned from her Army father.

Dingo huffed, jerked at the leash and pulled toward the exit.

"I know. We're going."

Dee was on the phone but held up her finger at them.

Sabine wandered over to a display that highlighted Dr. Lana's Complete Companion Sustenance. She cringed when she saw the price. One serving cost more than one meal at The Store. She grabbed the smallest treat bag and added it to her bill.

"Yes, ma'am. I understand. But I didn't make the appointment—our intern did." Dee rolled her eyes. "She will be told and we won't book anyone who does not live in this area. It won't happen again. Thank you." Dee firmly placed the phone on the desk and stuck her tongue at it.

"I didn't get y'all in trouble, did I?" Sabine asked contritely.

"Oh, fiddlesticks! I get in trouble with Madame Augustine almost daily. Ever since, Dr. Lana bought into the practice almost two years ago, she's been trying to make me quit. But as I said before, I think I know more about veterinary medicine than that jerk. She's a witch and he's an ass."

"Are they more than fellow animal lovers?"

"Sweetie, have you ever laid on eyes on Mavis Augustine?"

"No. Is she fugly?"

"Picture a Dallas Cowboy Cheerleader's head on a corpse with a spray tan."

"She's two colors? And looks like a skank? Is Dr. Lana is banging her?" Sabine did not engage the filter between her brain and mouth.

"Yes. Yes. I don't know. She's had a lot of plastic surgery to look like she's 22 years old. And enough spray tan to cover the entire state of Florida in orange goo. They're not living together but she is this practice's main investor so she tries to throw her weight around. And in a rude and overbearing manner. And I'm not altogether convinced she's actually human, what with all the silicone, Botox and toxic waste her plastic surgeon put in her face."

"Well this visit was a bust. I got nothing." Sabine liked Dee's moxie and stance in not being pushed around by Morticia and her mortician. That was the best way she could describe Madame Augstine and Dr. Lana. wailed. "Wasted time and wasted money. And he called me a dumb ass in Spanish."

"I don't think your visit was a waste." Dee's smile widened to a full grin. Her pupils erased the violet of her irises. For a moment, her whole body seemed to do a shimmy. "I called around and found out that Madame Skank didn't divorce the late Kirby Morgan nor did she report him missing. Now I'm no attorney but maybe there has got to be something dodgy going on with her not reporting him missing and with all the speculation that he is deceased."

Sabine opened her mouth and closed it. She was liking Dee more and more, to the point of considering her a kindred spirit.

Dee continued, "And when I get fussed at for making appointments for clients outside of this area and specifically Jaemore County, you better believe Madame Skank is acting suspiciously when her late husband's skeleton was found in the middle of nowhere."

"Well, it has officially been confirmed the remains found on his propery was actually him." Sabine, like the rest of the population, did not doubt the identity.

In a louder voice, Dee informed Sabine that the visit was $225. Dee looked over her shoulder before she handed Sabine her credit card back. "You better go. If Dr. Lana finds you still here, I won't have a job. I'll call you later after I make an anonymous phone call to Sally Jackson from Channel 7 to see if I can sic her on Mavis. I mean Madame Augustine."

Dingo and Sabine stepped into the sunshine. Surrounded by beautiful homes and the autumn trees, Sabine took a deep breath and stared down at Dingo. She had the most peculiar feeling that Dingo had saved her from a potential harmful visit. “Okay, you can have egg on your toaster. I'll suffer egg butt this time."

Dingo yawned and closed her eyes. Being noble and protecting her owner for the first time sucked the life from her.

-12-

Floating on a cloud while riding on a rainbow unicorn.

With her geocaching article's deadline looming, Sabine closeted herself in one of the bedrooms in her house away from the foul-smelling egg butt of her Aussie.

Sabine waived a photographer for this article and captured the pictures herself. She quickly downloaded all the recent pictures ending in the Winkie Park geocache and scrolled up, peering at each picture carefully.

"Nope. Nope. Maybe. Yes. Nope." Using her mouse, the photos swung by until one picture stood caught her eye. It was of the fake crime scene Newt contrived. Nothing but dirt, leaves and something that glinted from the flash. The next photo showed a bit more of the object. It looked cylindrical. It was probably just trash but with the intuition of a former investigative reporter for a major newspaper, Sabine couldn't silence her gut instinct. This was too close to a crime scene not to be important.

Sabine groped around for her phone and fast dialed Mia. "Hey, find a reason to go home. We need a pow-wow and we've got something to look for."

***

"Hello Sabine!" Mr. Wallis' voice boomed across the yard. As was his habit, he was reclining on his rocker on the covered front porch. But instead of his usual Sports Illustrated swimsuit issue, he held a paperback book entitled "Criminals: You Can't Live with 'Em and You Can't Incarcerate 'Em Forever."

"Come have a seat." He patted the other rocking chair. "You need to quiz me. This is my last class before I get my crime scene tech certificate from the Constantinople Academy of Criminal Justice in Kingston, Jamaica."

"Okay. Show me the questions."

Mr. Wallis pointed to a set of questions in the book marked as "revue section" while handing it over to Sabine.

"Revue? Doesn't that mean a parody? It should be spelled review."

"Yes. Let's review." Mr. Wallis nodded knowingly.

After yelling ten questions about fingerprints, blood splatter and drug testing, Mr. Wallis pronounced himself ready to test the next day. "Momma is in the kitchen. She's cooking up something for you and your gentleman caller's dinner. It's her Granny Lureen's chicken pot pie recipe. I'm just going to rest my eyeballs." He closed his eyes and started snoring almost immediately.

Sabine's mouth watered. Chicken pot pie. Practically its own food group on the nutritional pyramid.

"Sit." Mrs. Wallis pointed her spatula to one of the bar stools in the kitchen. "Mia went to go put some lipstick on to call Lee."

"She's skyping him?"

"No. She just wanted to look her best while she talked to him."

Sabine must have looked confused while she processed that statement.

"Don't try, baby girl. It'll just zap your brain cells."

Mia entered the kitchen, floating on a cloud while riding on a rainbow unicorn.

"Tone your glow down, moonbeam." Mrs. Wallis motioned. "We've got to plan. I've got your father studying for his final on the porch."

Mrs. Wallis poured some sweet tea and kneaded the pie dough while she related her information. Mrs. Wallis' task was to surreptitiously interrogate Lottie McCall who was Acting Director of the Community Management Association. The CMA, as it was known in the area, coordinated and dispensed all charitable activity. The non-profit was supported by all the local churches and had begun an outreach to the small business owners to tap for funds. In her capacity as her church's liaison to the charity and owner of the most successful real estate company in Jaemore County, Mrs. Wallis had the perfect angle to work.

"I got there yesterday midafternoon to drop of the church's check and Lottie did not look well."

Mia interrupted her mother. "Well you know Lottie has never been a happy person and that hair of hers...let's just say she went back for seconds when they were handing out ugly desserts."

Mrs. Wallis swatted at her daughter's hand with the spatula. "That may be true. Bless her heart, Lottie was never an attractive child but yesterday she looked positively ghoulish. No makeup and her hair had not been combed in days."

Mia sulked and rubbed her hand. Sabine knew exactly what Mia's thought process was. Lotta Hair's mane could only be described as hideous on good days. And if they were being honest, Mia's nemesis did have the most dreadful personality traits. She was rude, obnoxious and a penny-pincher both financially and in empathy. Lottie's manner was not the most desirable attribute for the director of such a well-loved helping charity in Jaemore County.

"Anyway." Mrs. Wallis set down a plate of lemon sugar cookies to accompany the sweet tea. "I asked Lottie what was wrong and she said she was getting over a bad case of strep throat. She also said Ms. Tilda is thinking about taking an extended vacation to Hilton Head because she came home after the dead Kirby outing to discover that her grandson Mick and Arial Bixby had been canoodling on her Louis XVI gold settee."

"I hope Mick stays sober and does right by Arial and her kids." Sabine felt she had a vested interest in Arial and Mick's success. She knew the two were working hard on their sobriety and being good parents.

"I think he's serious this time." Mrs. Wallis' eyes gleamed. "I've been holding this in all day. Arial was wearing the Dupont River Rock Lavalliere."

Sabine did a double take. "The River Rock what?"

"It's like a Y necklace made from sterling silver, freshwater pearls and one honking big ruby. It was one of the few things that have passed down from the DuPont family from before the Civil War." Mia crumpled her cookie impatiently at Sabine's ignorance. "The DuPonts were one of the three founding families of Jaemore County. The Jaemores and Greenleafs were the other two. Cinnamon Wallis was owned and freed by Glenda Wallis DuPont right before the Civil War. Glenda gave that necklace to Cinnamon but somehow." Mia used air quotes. "It got repo'ed by the Duponts who married into the Jaemores who married into the Greenleafs. It's all one big family tree full of poison ivy and kudzu. Trust me, Arial wearing this necklace is a big deal. It means Mick is serious about her."

"There's no quiz after this, right?" Sabine asked jokingly. "Anyway back to the subject at hand, I think it also means Lottie has given up on Mick ever noticing her. So she's not in a happy place."

Mrs. Wallis chewed a cookie slowly, "No. I just flat out asked her if she was upset about Kirby Morgan. And the girl had the nerve to clam up as if I was just asking for gossip's sake. She even took the church check and the real estate check before leaving the office. Rude girl. You're up." Mrs. Wallis pointed her spatula in her daughter's direction.

"I'm really ashamed of this." Mia hung her head with her hair covering her face. "PawPaw wouldn't talk to me about Kirby. He came to the door when I went to their house and he even said hello. But he clammed up tighter than a preacher in a whore house when I started mentioning all the ruckus about Kirby Morgan. OW! Mom stop hitting me with that spatula!"

"Quit being disrespectful. I know I taught you better than that."

"Anyway, before I was rudely abused by my mother, MeeMaw met me outside and said that PawPaw didn't actually hate Kirby. He was just disappointed that someone questioned his word. 'Cause everyone knows when PawPaw speaks or promises something, it's set in stone. Why Greenlanders ever thought PawPaw Lyons would lie about using Kirby's animals for meatloaf? And a few took Kirby's side in this. I didn't know but Hamilton Bilbo, that sleezy piece of roadkill, actually offered to file a lawsuit in civil court over PawPaw's "alleged use of unpaid meat." MeeMaw overheard Bilbo laying it on thick to Kirby over the kiwis and kumquats while she was picking up some white dirt at Dupont's Grocery." Dupont was the sole grocery store in the county and catered to its customers strange food habits.

"Bilbo would sell his own mama to make a buck." Sabine shivered at the thought of the slimy lawyer. "I always feel like I need a shower at the mention of his name."

"But right before I left, I talked with Elvis Lyons, June Bug's son." Mia put the last cookie back on the plate. Her appetite vanished with Sabine's opinion of Bilbo and her encounter with one of the youngest Lyons. "He was filthy and dirty and not in school as usual. He had a burlap sack and I made the mistake of asking what was in it. He reached into the bag to pull out a rabbit for The Diner's Wednesday's Mystery Meat dinner." Mia remembered the pride that gleamed on the young boy's face. "Elvis says he's been catching rabbits, possums and squirrels every week for three years since his grandparents insist on fresh meat and local ingredients. PawPaw pays him $10 an animal. So, if Elvis is to be believed, PawPaw has never served any...uh...less than native animals like the animals at the Morgan farm. And the next time someone has to go out the Lyons compound, it's not going to be me because that dead rabbit wouldn't stop staring at me."

The trio were silent for a moment and then Mrs. Wallis motioned for Sabine to divulge her information. When Sabine pulled out the print out of the newspaper picture of Kirby and Lotte, Mia erupted into laughter. After five minutes of Mia giggling at the possibility of Kirby and Lottie in love, Mrs. Wallis glowered sternly at her daughter to stop. It took the better part of fifteen minutes to relay the rest of the details including their new informant Dee's take on 'Madame Skank'. Finally, Sabine pulled out her phone to show the odd piece in the fake grave.

"I don't know if it's anything big but until we get a cause of death or anything more to go on, I vote we go out there and look under the peach tree."

Mia stomped her foot. "I can't go. I'm meeting Lee at Winkie Park for a cherry Icee."

"Amelia Juniper Wallis. Your sister is trying to keep your parents from going to jail. The very least you could do is go with her and be another set of eyes. I'm in the middle of cooking your dinners." Mrs. Wallis stood and checked the contents of the oven. "I don't mind going but we're going to have burnt pies if I do."

Sabine hurriedly reassured her that the chicken pot pies were more important than going to an old tree. There was no way she was going home without one of the best dishes in the county.

-13-

The pig was dead, not like that humongous worm.

Mia jutted out her lip like she was two years old. "I don't know why I have to go. This is your idea. I left my boots at the office and my Jimmy Choos are not really appropriate to go hiking. If they get scuffed..." Mia left the warning off.

"You'll do what? Make me pay? You've seen my bank balance. And it's a $225 lighter after yesterday. Is there an expense account to go along with this investigation that I don't know about? And what if Newt has to arrest your dad for something that we could've prevented?"

Mia threw up her hands as if Sabine had no clue how valuable her shoes were and the amount they set back her bank account. Truth to be told, Sabine didn't know and really had no desire to know.

The peach tree draped against a magnificent Georgia afternoon sun. Mrs. Wallis had said tree was a Summer Flame variety and Sabine could make out a few red autumn leaves clinging to the branches. The tarp was gone but Sabine had no problem finding where Newt had it. Though the tree was a good fifteen feet tall, it didn't cover a wide area so Sabine picked up a stick and cautiously poked around the trunk. She had taken Drayton's venomous snake warning to heart.

"Here it is!" Mia whooped triumphantly. She pointed a finger at the grimy item. "Looks like an old school paste container. But I'm not getting it. I see a worm nearby and I just got my manicure repaired from the last time I hung out with you."

"Oh my God, Mia, really?" Sabine lined the stick up with the worm and tossed toward her friend. "It's a worm. It's not exactly dangerous. And anyway, didn't you tell me you tried that Glorioso Red Pie from the Italian restaurant in Athens? You said it tasted okay but you found out it's made from pork blood!"

"Well..." Mia groped for the right words to defend herself. "Lee said he liked a girl who was not afraid of adventure. And the pig was dead, not like that humongous worm thing you threw at me."

"Whatever." Sabine grabbed a twig and poked at the plastic bag holding the dirty cylinder. "I know what this is. It looks like an old epinephrine syringe. It's the medicine you jab in your thigh if you're having a severe allergic reaction. I can't make out the name on the prescription but it's a Dupont Store Pharmacy item. I can see four of the six prescription numbers. The plastic bag has degraded too much and the name is wearing off."

"So?"

"That's your answer? So?" Sabine felt her heart race. "Remember Snookie brought the arm with a medical alert bracelet with Kirby's name. Drayton said Kirby had a deathly allergy to bees! What if this is Kirby's EpiPen? Why would Kirby's EpiPen be fifty yards from where they found him?"

"Maybe he was always losing things. Maybe he drank too much moonshine. Maybe he died of fright because he saw Old Lady Hughes' boobs flappin' in the breeze. Or maybe it's not even his!" Mia fussed. Her accent was becoming pronounced which meant she was getting annoyed.

"Sabine, as much as I love trying to keep my parents from bein' charged with a murder or any crime, it's important to note that Kirby's cause of death has not been released. You're makin' a leap of...insanity...in callin' this a murder. Right now, it's just a corpse with a name. Quit puttin' felonies or even misdemeanors in my head. I'm gonna have nightmares tonight about worms and bees." With that Mia stomped off to the Challenger to mulishly wait for Sabine.

Sabine was indecisive. If her discovery was evidence, Newt wouldn't want her to touch the items. Her quandary was to leave it and take a chance with the items getting lost or taking them to Newt. In the end, she took a clearer picture of the bag and gently covered it back up.

***

"Vubkis." Newt ground out after checking a text later that evening.

"Is that a new drink like *Brännvin*? 'Cause I have to tell you, my taste buds were off for two weeks after drinking that." Sabine stopped petting Dingo and shuddered at the memory of the strong Swedish version of vodka. Dingo glowered at her, perturbed that her owner halted her massage.

"*Nej*." Newt answered distractedly. "The *attans* medical examiner could not find a *jävla* cause of death for Morgan."

Sabine knew when Newt dropped Swedish phrases and profanity, the situation was never good. This made her nervous to broach the subject of her discovery with him. She did not want to add more fuel to his mood about her poking her nose into the investigation.

"There was no blunt force trauma, no broken bones, nothing. Just a skull and a few ribs." Newt put the phone down and released a sigh of frustration. "I don't even know a crime was committed. Mrs. Morgan said Kirby was taking an extended trip to Africa the last time she saw him the day he disappeared to replenish his stock before the exterminator came out to the farm. And it was verified by a friend who was with her at the same time. We have a body and nothing else. Vupkis! "

"Bupkis! Okay. I get it. You don't have squat." Sabine clarified. She took a deep breath and said in rush. "Mia and I did find what looked like an epinephrine prescription under the peach tree where you put the tarp. Drayton said Kirby was deathly allergic to bees."

"And?" Newt began rubbing Dingo's ears. Dingo rolled over in rapturous ecstasy and had the gall to moan with pleasure.

"Well, why would his EpiPen be so far away from his body? If I was that close to anaphylactic shock, I'd make sure I had that. Newt, something's off. I just know it." Sabine was relieved at his reaction to her news.

Newt stopped scratching the dog for a moment and knit his blue eyes together. "So you and Mia are sticking your *näsa* into things that you should not. Aren't you?"

Sabine hemmed and hawed before she answered. Her state of relief evaporated. "If *näsa* means intelligence, then yes. I just don't want to see either Mr. or Mrs. Wallis get the book thrown at them."

"One—I don't even have a crime and you're trying to clear people who I think as my extended family. I know something happened but there's nothing there." Newt tried to tamper his agitation. "Second—didn't you learn anything when you confronted a meth dealer armed with a knife and all you had was a handful of ragweed?

"But the bright side was that you came charging to my rescue like Galahad?" Sabine cut her eyes at her knight. "And we did record Mia singing the theme to Gilligan's Island on the morphine drip for her broken ankle. It went viral on YouTube."

"Yeah, good times by all." Newt had calmed down enough to resume scratching Dingo. "Don't go looking for any trouble when there's none."

Sabine shoved the Aussie off the couch and scooted closer. "I think Dingo has been scratched enough."

"Trying to change the subject?" Newt's mood shifted. Despite the times he could be ready to wring Sabine's neck for her antics, she always managed to make him laugh.

"Is it working?' Sabine tilted her head to the side, broadened her smile, and gave him her best seductive look.

"For now, but you'll have to apologize later to Dingo for pushing her away." Newt pulled Sabine up to lead her to the bedroom.

-14-

A bump in the pregnancy rate in the area, probably due to the free peach moonshine.

Sabine was at loose ends. Helen had curtly acknowledged the column about geocaching for the magazine's next edition. Her newspaper article about Kirby was submitted even with the scant information. The *Jaemore Journal* publisher promised her the article would edge out the latest local news on the continued vandalism of the Baptist church cemetery and the new gossip column penned by a dubious reporter named "Chet Chat." Sabine had informed the newspaper for the umpteenth time that Snookie Wallis the Wienie Dog was the digger and not some encroaching grave robbers from Atlanta. She also pointed out that Chet

Chat frequently wrote outright lies and innuendo about the more prominent citizens of the area.

A random thought tried to coalesce in her memory. Sabine replayed her conversations with Dee, Mia, and Mrs. Wallis. Mrs. Wallis gave a check to Lottie McCall. No, she gave two—one from the church and the other from Mrs. Wallis' real estate business. Then it struck. Real estate. Who now owns Kirby Morgan's farm? Now that Kirby's been dead, does his wife inherit?

A quick internet search uncovered that the Farm had been in foreclosure six months after Kirby's disappearance and had been bought at auction by a West Coast firm named Zephyr Limited. Sabine sifted through the legalese swiftly and saw that most of the assets of the farm were also auctioned. One entry caught her eye.

"One single wide mobile home manufactured in 1998. Condition: fair with considerable wear on inside carpet. Served as the business office of farm. Color of mobile home: Fuchsia. 2 BR/1BA." Sabine read out loud. "Fuchsia? Is that in the pink family?"

Dingo halted her study of the terroristic chipmunks near the driveway to stare at Sabine positive her owner lacked the mental capacity to extrapolate data.

"Stop staring at me." Sabine snarled. "Not all humans are as smart as Australian Shepherds."

Fuchsia. She had seen a bright color on a building somewhere in Jaemore County. Mia would know, but Sabine hated to call her at work, especially since they were bickering. Who else besides a Wallis would know Jaemore County? What other person would proudly proclaim themselves a native?

Edweener Bumpus Ostermeyer. Edweener was a great source about the area's dying moonshine industry for Sabine's first article she wrote in the Dixie Days magazine. Her 'grampus,' the sheriff of Jaemore County during Prohibition in the 1920's, was the area's finest supplier of illegal alcohol. Edweener had also just recently rekindled a romance with the current inept sheriff, Jim "call me Ostie" Ostermeyer. Sabine's first encounter with the sheriff had been when she found an unconscious Arial Bixby in one of Edweener's rental trailers. That was also the first day she met Newt.

Trailers! The thought finally jumped to the forefront. One of Edweener's trailers on Vondale Circle was a horrible fuchsia color. Surely there were not two ghastly colored trailers in the area.

A text to Edweener confirmed that the Vondale trailer had been, in fact, bought at the auction for the farm. Sabine could pick up the key at Edweener's favorite poker place, Maxi's Pad.

"I'll see you later, Dingo. I'm going to make a case come hell or high water."

***

Despite living in Jaemore County for a year, Sabine had never had the inclination to enter the area's oldest drinking and carousing establishment, Maxi's Pad, or the neighboring business, a fishing and tackle supplier called the Master Baits. The owners were parishioners of Sabine's church in

Athens, but they had not formally met. Her only knowledge of the Masters was gathered through local gossip and the Greenleaf Journal. The local newspaper had featured the Masters because of their support of the local school district. Maxi and Matthew Master had started their businesses twenty years ago when they won a few millions in one of the Georgia lottery games.

The parking lot to Maxi's Pad's was filled with assorted motorcycles, large working trucks, and a rickety recreational vehicle with the words "Master Baits, Jaemore's #1 Dealer of Fishing Supplies" painted on the side. Planted next to it was another business sign singing the praises of the "Maxi Master Tax Preparation Service and Handy Girl Contractors." Positioned to the right of the RV was Edweener's large pickup with her horse trailer attached. Sabine parked on the other side of the RV. Though technically a vehicle, it had not moved from its spot in all the time Sabine lived in Jaemore County so it was reasonably safe from other traffic.

It took a few moments for Sabine's eyes to adjust to the darkness of the bar. Three customers were engaged in a heated game of darts while a lone man leaned against the bar staring at his whiskey pensively. Sabine recognized Matthew Master standing behind the bar watching a YouTube video of a NASCAR race, cheering on Kyle Busch.

"I need two cards. Two cards from the top or I'll beat the ever lovin' crap out of you, Dickie Lyons." Edweener Bumpus' voice bellowed over the television and dart game. Edweener glanced up and spied Sabine. "Jus' a minute. Lemme clean up here and I'll talk to ya, Sabine."

When Sabine first met Edweener, the image of Jed Clampett wearing a granny's nightgown and curlers popped into her head. Edweener had been the landlord to Arial Bixby and more or less watched out for Arial's kids, Dion and Kayla. Sabine was convinced during her first encounter on Edweener's property the woman raised murderous chickens and psychotic pigs.

Sabine almost fainted from the sight, but Edweener had turned out to be a redneck fairy godmother in the end. A devout gambler, she traveled around the South looking for blackjacks and lucky dice. It was profitable for her, also. She handily won a regional poker competition and walked out with a cool million. Unbeknownst to Arial, Edweener had set up a college fund for Dion and Kayla and funded a new scholarship program at Jaemore County High School.

Edweener had married her high school sweetheart, Sheriff Ostermeyer. Their wedding was a camouflaged themed extravaganza at Winkie Park in July. The event lasted two days. There was a bump in the pregnancy rate in the area, probably due to the free peach moonshine supplied by the bride's family. Sabine was honored to be the maid of honor and Dingo was ring bearer—a task that the dog performed with grace, unlike her owner who tripped and almost fell into the pond filled with duck poop and scum.

Sabine perched herself on a barstool and ordered a Diet Dr Pepper, easy ice, and picked through the pretzels aimlessly.

"Hey, Sabine!" Edweener enveloped her in a bear hug and sat precariously on a neighboring stool. "I got the key. I've been busier than a one-legged cat in a sandbox since me and Ostie got back from the Gulf Shores. I plum forgot that I bought that trailer from the county tax auction. I never got 'round to cleaning it out proper like since I bought it. Yore be careful, yer hear? Ain't been out there since we loaded the chickens and Hoss the pig last summer. No renters yet." She passed the key to Sabine. "So, girlie, how are you and that poleece man? Y'all gonna ever git hitched? Or is it gonna be a shotgun wedding?" Edweener guffawed loudly and slurped her water. "Gimme another one, Matt."

"Why are you drinking water? Isn't moonshine your...wait a moment...are you..." Sabine's voice dropped to a horrified whisper. "Are you pregnant?"

Edweener's face transformed into an expression of disbelief. "No, ma'am. I ain't got a bun in the oven. I just ain't a drinker while playin' poker. Messes with your poker face."

"Oh. I'm sorry. I just assumed..." Sabine let the apology hang.

Edweener started to cackle. "Wouldn't that be someum? Ostie would poot a brick. My ma and granny all had babies up until their fifties so it'd be a good trick to play on Ostie. He..."

A scream erupted from the dart game. Two drunken men decided to act out their latent William

Tell tendencies and throw a pocketknife at a partially filled beer bottle located on the third friend's head. The knife had toppled over the beer can which caused it to splash onto the floor, inciting an earsplitting caterwaul from the poker players.

"Sabine, yore better git out and do what ya need to do at Kirby's trailer. I'll get the key back later. This is gonna be a bad fight. You just don't go wasting good beer like that."

-15-

It should have been considered a tool in the Spanish Inquisition.

Edweener's three derelict trailers drooped alarmingly to the left. It was clear that the ties holding the trailers to the ground had degraded. Sabine's eyes immediately zoomed in on the faded fuchsia one in the middle. A flashback of ferocious chickens attacking Sabine zipped through her mind. Fortunately, Edweener had moved all her animals to Ostie's family homestead on the other side of the county. No pigs were threatening to stampede on her, and no chickens would peck at her like the first time she visited.

Why the door was locked when all of the windows were open, Sabine had no idea. But when the door swung open, mildew and mold together with animal droppings made a smell so bad it should have been considered a tool in the Spanish Inquisition.

Sabine hopped over the holes in the floor but halted to cock her ear to what sounded like rats scratching in the corner of the kitchen.

"Oh, Kirby probably didn't keep anything in the kitchen anyway." Sabine decided resolutely and headed the opposite way to the bedroom. The biggest bedroom still held a makeshift desk from two sawhorses and a door laid across it. The closet revealed a few grimy dress shirts and an empty bureau. A peek in the smaller bedroom revealed a small twin-size bed that had been used as a nest by unknown rodents.

Sabine rifled through the remaining papers to no avail. Silverfish fled as she disrupted their dinners. A few to-do lists in a cramped, unfamiliar handwriting and some faded newspapers were all that remained. Sabine grabbed the first sheet dated three days before he was last seen and read.

"Call the allergist. Visit the William Harris Homestead re: materials used in restoration of cellar. Call for pests. Talk to the Ass." Sabine stopped and reread the last item. "Talk to the Ass? As in a mule? I know a lot of people in this county who could be called an ass. What or who do you mean Kirby?"

Sabine whipped out her camera from the back pocket of her jeans and began to snap pictures of the list. She really needed to go home. The Diet Dr

Pepper had already made its way down so her first priority was a toilet. Preferably a clean working one.

The bathroom in this trailer was a no go as she glanced in the only one. It was a bit filthy. Although the fixtures seemed in good repair, Sabine doubted the plumbing functioned. She also had left the computer on at home and Dingo had probably ordered ten cartons of Yummy Good Treats in bacon and cheese online. A mental list of her cupboard also revealed a necessary trip to the grocery store and an ice-cold bottled water topped that list.

***

Of all the things Sabine thought she'd see in front of her home that late afternoon, a spotted miniature donkey stripping the leaves from her favorite Joseph's Coat rose was not even on her wildest bucket list. When another brown one about 3 feet tall moseyed toward the Challenger, Sabine knew karma was bitch slapping her for enrolling Old Lady Hughes in the Sex Toy of the Month club.

From the raucous racket inside, Dingo was feverishly attempting a prison break to herd or possibly train the donkeys to serve her. Just as Sabine was debating whether or not she needed a shot of Edweener's moonshine, Newt, sporting a black eye, scurried down the porch waving his arms like he was an NFL referee calling offside.

"I know. I know." Newt huffed when he skidded to a stop by the Challenger. "They're evidence in an investigation and we don't have any place to keep them. The evidence room is a locked broom closet and Dickie Lyons kicked up a fuss when he saw them in the cell over from him."

"Newton Johansson. I swear to God you are in such deep doodoo now." Sabine, having lost her apprehension of the donkeys, slammed her door shut and marched toward the spotted one enjoying a rosebud salad with a donkey balsamic slobber.

Newt hurriedly manhandled the donkeys into the fenced backyard, wincing at the strident howling by an angry canine flinging herself against the front door.

After hitting the bathroom to wipe the worst of the dirt from the trailers and locking the dog in the bedroom, Sabine immediately popped the top on a cold Shiner Black Lager imported straight from Shiner, Texas. She coveted the small supply and only partook for situations that required a special drink. She held her hand up and guzzled, relishing in the coolness of the brew.

"Okay. Now I'm ready." Sabine suppressed a belch.

"It started out that Dickie Lyons and Edweener Bumpus were locked in mortal combat over a game of..." Newt paused from putting the contents of the grocery bag into the cupboard and pulled his notebook from his jeans back pocket. "A game of Omaha High-low Mixed at Maxi's Pad. Dickie had one too many beers which meant he had one so he was gunning to win. When Edweener called his bluff, he bet the rest of his late father's belongings, namely those two donkeys outside on our front lawn."

Sabine pinched the bridge of her nose and contemplated whether or not Shiner Lager mixed well with Swedish vodka.

"Edweener drove Dickie to the Lyons compound to get the donkeys. June Bug finds out and lets loose on Dickie who was about to pass out from his lone beer. June Bug told Edweener to leave the barn where the donkeys were kept, but Edweener already called the sheriff's office. Apparently, the two donkeys were sleeping in two bathtubs in a barn which is illegal in Georgia. I know because I looked it up."

"Newt, I'm still not seeing why we are hosting two donkeys. Where is Animal Control?"

"I'm getting there. June Bug took a swing at Dickie after I showed up. Dickie ducked. I didn't. June Bug turned red and burst out crying. When Dickie got back up, he thought I had hit his mother and he tried to pull my hair. Dean, the road deputy, pulled up right then and handcuffed the drunk Dickie. Before Dean could shut the backdoor of my cruiser, Dickie was already passed out on the backseat. And since the donkeys were sleeping in bathtubs, we called Lee Kingsley who is the only official I know with a trailer. Animal Control happily told me that since the donkeys were evidence in a crime, they were bowing out of taking them. Basically, I became the foster father to a pair of donkeys."

"You are making this crap up." Sabine covered her mouth to stop giggling. The beer had done its duty in giving her the needed buzz to relax her.

Newt grinned. "I couldn't make this up. It was Edweener's idea to confiscate the donkeys and since it was illegal for the donkeys to bed down in a bathtub, we took them. We put the donkeys in the holding cell next to Dickie. When he regained sobriety from his inebriated state, he started screaming his head off about the donkeys staring him down. Lee had to pull himself off a call about a boat in a tree near the highway to transport them here."

"We have two donkeys who are vital evidence in a...is it a felony?" Sabine mentally played connect the dots with all of Newt's details. Somehow, she missed the boat in a tree part or maybe she'd become so accustomed to quirkiness of Greenleaf it did not phase her.

Newt shrugged. "I don't know if it's a misdemeanor or felony but it's some crazy *skit*. If I had to go back to the office one more time today, I'm quitting, and I'll be a stay at home whatever you need me to be. And by the way, the jenny is named Willy and the jack is Jack."

"What the hell?" Sabine's buzz dissipated and the idea of the Swedish Vodka was becoming more enticing.

"A jenny is a female donkey. Her name is Willy. A jack is a male donkey and his name is Jack."

"Get the *Brännvin* ready. Dingo is gonna need a belt too after seeing the donkeys. Then sit down and I'll tell you about my find." Sabine was half-way to the kitchen to get two large tea glasses. This day did not call for a shot, but a big tumbler.

Newt poured his drink and splayed out on the couch. "Okay. Hit me."

Sabine outlined what she had discovered in her quick search of Kirby's old trailer. "He's got some stuff over there. Like old clothes and some paperwork." She looked at the bottom of her empty glass. Despite her insistence, Newt refused to fill it to the brim but only poured about two fingers of the vodka. "I'm gonna need more."

Before Sabine could polish off her second round, a terse knock on the door caused Dingo to ram the bedroom door so hard, it knocked down Sabine's Aggie pennant from the wall.

Edweener stood on the front porch in all her redneck, Jed Clampett glory and was toting a large briefcase.

"Hey Sabine. Can I talk to you an' your fella?"

"Sure." Sabine motioned for her to come and shuddered at the smell of cigarette smoke that followed Edweener. "Have a seat." Please not the couch she prayed, sit in Newt's ugly orange Naugahyde recliner. Sabine breathed a sigh of relief mixed with second hand smoke when her guest plopped down in the recliner.

Without ado, Newt handed a clear glass of *Brännvin* to Edweener and released Dingo from her bedroom prison. Edweener and Dingo were old friends.

"Well if it ain't my buddy, Dingo. How ya doin' girl?" After a few moments of scratching, Edweener set her glass down and Dingo took a slurp of the vodka. She burped and promptly fell asleep at Edweener's feet.

"Fine dawg you got there Sabine."

"Yeah. She's oodles of love and respect." Sabine managed to inject a false note of sincerity in her voice. Sabine loved that dog of hers, but it seemed she was the only one to notice Dingo was not an angel 100% of the time. If she were honest with herself,

Dingo possessed vastly superior intelligence than her owner. "What brings you out here?"

"Newt, I gotta say. I don't want the donkeys. Ain't got a place for them with all my pigs and chickens. Me and Ostie don't got the room in the house."

Newt nodded. "Okay, so why the fuss about the donkey in the bathtubs?"

"Well, Dickie made a bet and he's gotta pay the piper! Ain't nuthin' lower than a man not payin' his debts." Edweener seethed. "And I gots to thinkin'. Since y'all weren't here when Kirby disappeared and Sabine made that connection to the trailer I got at auction, I thoughts to meself, 'Newt's gotta know this.'" She paused to take a long draught of *Brännvin* from the same cup Dingo had imbibed from. "Right good and somethin' light so I don't get all giggly and drunk."

Edweener leaned back and continued. "Kirby came up to my trailer a few days 'afore he took off. Seems he wanted to start a pettin' zoo and heard how friendly my pig, Hoss, was. I 'member it. All frou-frou with his suit and briefcase. I thoughts to meself that he was one good-lookin' high-falutin' man to go inspectin' pigs and chicks. You know Sabine, you've met 'im, too. Hoss likes to get in the mud and play."

Sabine's face froze. That Hoss was responsible for chasing her down like a prize sow at the Texas State Fair last April and the chickens pecked at her and had the audacity to chase her.

"Well's, Kirby tells me he already bought two donkeys—them the same ones y'all gots back in the yard I 'pect. They escaped during the break-in. I reckon they got captured, probably by Elvis, that little Lyons boy who needs a good kick in his britches."

"Okay. Where does that leave us, Edweener?" Newt motioned wishing he could play wrap-up music to get Edweener to her point of being in his recliner.

"'Cause on account of Kirby's dead body and Mavis gettin' pretty ugly with him right afore he split."

Sabine didn't have to glance at Newt. "Edweener, what did Mavis do?"

"Ostie didn't tell ya? I love that man of mine but I swears that man sometimes doesn't know to scratch his watch or wind his ass. Him and me were talking right after you left. He comes in to Maxi's to eat fifty cent chicken wings on Wednesday on account it being so close to the jail and he ain't driving still. And PawPaw's mystery meat on Wednesday tastes close to squirrel. I tolds him about you wantin' to look through the trailer and he says," Edweener deepened her voice to mimic Ostie. "'I called down there to 'Lanta to check on Mavis and a friend o' hers says Kirby had taken off to Africa or Asia to buy some more weird food.'"

Newt shifted impatiently and was irritated that Ostie called Mavis. He had been trying to track the elusive woman down for days. Ostie was notorious for not giving Newt details that could be beneficial in an investigation. He was pretty sure Ostie didn't get the name of the person he spoke with about Kirby. For the life of him, Newt couldn't figure out why the voters of Jaemore County kept reelecting Ostie. The sheriff was nice enough but lacked the common sense needed for a public safety position. "Edweener, I still have to feed the donkeys so can you get to the point?"

But Edweener was not to be rushed. "When that man came out to buy some animals, he gots a phone call that someone had broken in and all his animals stampeded out. He left lickety split but he forgot his briefcase. He never came back for it. So today after I meets up with Sabine and talk to Ostie, I remember that Kirby accidental left his papers for me, so here they are." Edweener opened the briefcase and grabbed a handful of papers. She thrust them toward Newt. "I know that Kirby was servin' her with a cease and desist order for defamation. Them papers are here in this case. Now that Kirby is dead, he ain't gonna need them." With another gulp, Edweener burped unbecomingly.

"Wait...wait...wait." Sabine held her hand up and flashed a glanced at Newt who was looking more and more interested in Edweener's tale. "Defamation?"

"Ya doan know? That means telling lies about someone or their business. I knowed 'cause someone did that to my grampus back in the day saying his peach lightning was not ho-made."

"Edweener, I know what defamation is." Sabine stuttered. "What has it got to with Mavis and Kirby?

"Oh, she's the one who defamationed him." Edweener's eye bugged out and her upper lip tightened. She put the briefcase on the floor in front of Sabine.

Sabine was sure she sat there in her living room gob smacked for a good two minutes. Even Newt couldn't control the incredulous expression on his face.

Edweener, to her credit, reclined the chair as far as it would go and settled down with the vodka in one hand and her other scratching a sleepy Dingo. She nodded toward the case near Sabine's feet.

"There's them records in that bag there." Edweener grinned. "Lordy! Yore should see your faces. Didn't know that Edweener Edith Bumpus had it in her to surprise someone, didja?"

Sabine leaned forward and opened the top of the satchel briefcase. She reached inside and pulled as many papers as her hand could grasp. Sure enough, the petition for a cease and desist order that outlined Kirby's case for defamation was there. She began reading out loud for Newt's sake. Newt had started pacing. Kirby alleged that Mavis falsely and deliberately slandered his business by informing various high-end restaurants in Atlanta and Savannah of deplorable conditions at the Exotic Animal Farm. According to an affidavit by Anthony Gatsby, owner and chef of Gatsby's on the River, Mavis Augustine Morgan let it slip during one night during a meet and mingle for a museum fundraiser that her husband routinely starved animals and used questionable hormone injections to bolster growth.

In addition to the defamation paperwork, Sabine rifled through a rough draft of a petition for divorce as Kirby Morgan as the petitioner in the Fulton County Superior Court. Sabine scanned through it noting Kirby was merely asking for a "no-fault" divorce which basically meant both parties don't want to be married any longer.

It was also interesting to know that Kirby was being represented by none other than Hamilton Bilbo, Esquire. Hamilton was a combination of the arrogance of Napoleon, the scruples of Billy the Kid and the countenance of a redneck Romeo with questionable intelligence. His ability to hit on any female within ten miles of Greenleaf was legendary. Sabine counted her stars when Mia informed her of Hamilton's sleezy ways before she had the misfortune to accept a date with him.

Newt rubbed his stubble on his chin. "Mavis and Kirby were getting a divorce and Mavis was bad mouthing Kirby to his potential clients?"

"Yup. That ain't all. Before Kirby left, he tole me that he knowed Mavis was messin' around with an ass and he had the proof. And I doan think she was messin' with one of those donkeys 'cause that'd be too damn gross." Edweener predicted.

Newt inspected the papers for a few minutes while Edweener polished off the vodka and scratched her belly.

"This puts more teeth in the suspicion that Kirby could have been murdered." Newt smiled at Edweener. With his Swedish accent, it came out as Edveener. "But you have to tell me how you knew it was illegal to keep donkeys in a bathtub in the state of Georgia."

"Oh, that's a story." Edweener held out her glass for a refill. "In the Bad Times—that's what my Grampus Bumpus called the 1920's when yore couldn't buy likker—Ms. Tilda's pa, Tedmund Greenleaf, told two Yankee revenuers where Grampus' and Grampma's stills were. That

Tedmund was lower than a snake in a wagon's rut and they were always at each other's throats since Grampus won the blue ribbon at the 1928 County Fair.

One of Grampus' friends found out and tole 'em. My pa poured out the batch of lightning into a bathtub afore they gots there. Grampma had the idea of putting their mean donkey Cletus in there so the revenuers wouldn't get too close on account of Cletus might bite them. Well it worked and the revenuers left with nothing but the sight of Grampma cleaning the backside of an ornery jackass." Edweener bent forward, eager to relate the tale.

"Tedmund gots so mad he called one of his buddies in 'Lanta and they doan passed that law. That's why too you can't trust anyone who goes out of their way to take someone's likker away from 'em, especially with Yankees. That's why I gots upset when them guys spilt that beer today at Maxi's Pad. Good likker is hard to come by." Edweener finished her story with a dramatic flourish, scratched Dingo one more time and walked steadily to the front door. Not a wobble, bobble, or slight stagger in her step. Edweener pushed the front door and made her exit. She'd accomplished the purpose for her visit.

"'Good likker is hard to come by'. Sounds like a bad fortune cookie. And after two belts of my *Brännvin*, I'd think she'd be plastered, but she's stone cold sober." Newt commented. He twisted around when Sabine answered with a gentle snore, knocked out by her one bottle of beer and two shots of *Brännvin* . Newt shook his head and smiled. He thought moving to Greenleaf was a good decision but taking the first step to get to know Sabine was the best one. In all his life, he never planned on falling in love with strong, independent woman who could make him laugh so much. Sabine was headstrong especially when she saw injustice. He also was a bit scared when she disregarded her safety as she pursued her quest to make the world a better place.

-16-

It's pronounced 'knee' not 'neigh' like a horse.

Sabine pried one eye open and gagged. Dingo was splayed across Newt's pillow on her back asleep with her bottom two inches from Sabine's nose.

Sabine shifted her body carefully, hoping not to aggravate her pounding head.

"And she's awake." Newt called softly from the bathroom. "You slept eleven hours. For the first four hours, you didn't move. I thought about taking you to the hospital. But I changed my mind and we're going to call the world record people to confirm you as the world's fastest intoxication on the least amount of alcohol. One beer and two shots? Really?"

"Quit yelling. And Tucker got plastered on one beer." Sabine shut her eyes. "What time is it?"

"6:45 Thursday morning. Do you remember anything from last night?"

Sabine pondered for a moment and grunted. "Edweener came over? Something about Kirby taking a bath in peach lightning?"

"Something like that." Newt sauntered over and kissed her forehead. "I scanned the documents and you can look at them when you feel human again. I should know better and trust those investigative reporter instincts that there may be a crime."

It took a full hour for Sabine to muster the energy to sit up. "Stop looking at me like I'm a lush." Sabine fussed at Dingo who stared at her reproachfully. "You should have a hangover, too, since you drank that acid Newt calls vodka." Sabine felt Dingo's disapproving gaze on her while she held her pounding head between her hands.

Dingo didn't deign to reply. She flicked her stub and strolled out of the bedroom, no doubt feeling superior to her owner. A few moments later, Sabine heard the telltale whimpering that signaled someone was in the house and scratching Dingo's belly.

"Sabine, what is wrong with you?" Mrs. Wallis sauntered into the bedroom.

"I drank a beer and two shots of stuff New calls vodka last night."

Mrs. Wallis peered over and then took a step back. "You look like you've been rode hard and put up wet. Go take a shower and I'll mix up Granny Lureen's hangover drink." She turned on her heel and left to make Granny's concoction.

Five minutes passed before Sabine rolled out of bed and stood. The shower helped but Sabine readily took the headache pills and the infamous Wallis' cure-all for hangovers that resembled the swamp algae and smelled suspiciously like lemons.

"Drink it all. You should know better than to mix beer with liquor." Mrs. Wallis commented while she cleaned up the kitchen.

When Sabine spied Mrs. Wallis putting away a lemon scented disinfectant, she shrugged. She didn't care what was in the concoction it as long as it stopped her stomach from gurgling and head from pounding.

"So when are you going to tell me about you and Mia not talking to each other?" Mrs. Wallis with her hands on her hips towered above Sabine.

Sabine subconsciously shrunk into her chair. "I don't know what I did. Mia's been snappish all week. It started when she threatened Newt. She said she'd get Mr. Wallis to break us up and then she fussed at me when we went to the farm the day you were cooking the chicken pot pies."

"Well I think something's up and it's not a good up." Mrs. Wallis predicted. "Drink up, baby girl. We're going to visit Mavis Augustine. She is selling her house and there's an agent tour going on. Mia can't get off work so it's you and me."

*****

Sabine shifted uncomfortably in the rock hard bus seat belonging to the Scarlett Cato Real Estate Office. She was wearing an itchy camisole bra and the lace rubbed painfully on her back.

"Quit squirming." Mrs. Wallis hissed.

"My back is itching."

Mrs. Wallis palmed her a pen and Sabine was able to reach the offending spot. When that was satisfied, Sabine concentrated on the speaker's well-modulated voice.

"I'm Courtneigh La Fay but you can call me Neigh. That's N-E-I-G-H." A blonde beanpole motioned toward the scrolling LED sign that surrounded the luxurious bus. "Thank you for making the drive to attend the Scarlett Cato Real Estate Tour of Greater Buckhead for the Homes of Tomorrow." The lithe, overly enthusiastic voice of a junior agent grated on Sabine's nerves.

While the hangover was gone thanks to Granny Lureen, Sabine flinched when Courtneigh accented every other word. When the agent went on to gush about the amazing opportunity each visitor had, Sabine spied fake tears in her eyes.

Sabine raised her hand. "Excuse me, Neigh."

"It's pronounced 'knee' not 'neigh' like a horse." Neigh cast a withering look at the obvious country bumpkin.

"Well, when I read on your name lit up on the sign like a Las Vegas freak show, it's spelled like what a horse would say. My apologies." Sabine cooed insincerely. "I just wanted to know how many houses do we get to see today."

Neigh replied in a contemptuous tone. "If you bothered to read your folder, you'd know we have four houses and two penthouses on the schedule." With her pert nose in the air, she dismissed Sabine.

Sabine childishly stuck out her tongue and started silently chanting, “Neigh, Neigh, Ms. La Fey is gonna pay” to the tune of Crazy by Patsy Cline.

"The first house is a historical beauty. It is owned by a descendant of a friend of the Stovall family. General Marcellus Stovall of the Confederate States of America was the hero of the Battle of Chickamauga in 1863 where he led his troops to a victory of Union forces. General Stovall had settled down nearby in Augusta after the war and made a living in cotton."

"Why is that important?" Sabine leaned over to Mrs. Wallis.

"Because who your people are can be a powerful selling tool." Mrs. Wallis whispered back. "Take Cinnamon Wallis. She was a former slave who ran the Underground Railroad in Greenleaf along with her friend, Glenda Wallis Dupont. One of the reasons Micah got so much from that land was because it belonged to Glenda Dupont who willed it to Cinnamon. The Wallis’ owned all the land for the peach trees and the Duponts owned the businesses in town including that huge manor that Lee bought. Don’t you remember Mia’s lecture? Duponts are a big name in our area."

Neigh halted her speech and stared at Mrs. Wallis and Sabine.

"Oh, honey lips. I'm sorry. My associate doesn't understand any history." Mrs. Wallis pasted a false smile on her face. "I was explaining the tactics used by the Confederate Army at the Battle of Chickamauga in 1863."

"That's fine. Anything to educate the ignorant, I suppose. As I was saying, this house is in the highly desirable Tuxedo Road with almost seven full acres. Nine bedrooms, seven full baths and two powder rooms. It was built in 1870 by a daughter of General Stovall's best friend at West Point before the War of Northern Aggression. Immaculate condition. And only $9.5 million!"

Neigh held on to a strap as the bus made a sharp left and screeched to halt at an ornate gate. The realtor stepped out of the bus in impossibly thin and high stilettos to press a speaker button.

When Neigh reboarded the bus, she had a look of utter ecstasy on her face. From Sabine's view, she half believed Neigh had an encountered the Virgin Mary and was basking in adoration. Just when Sabine was about to break out her rosary, Neigh spoiled it and spoke in her upper crust Southern drawl.

"We are in luck! The butler informed me that the esteemed owner, Ms. Mavis Augustine, is here and we may be able to talk with her!" Neigh clasped her hands together as if in rapturous worship in front of piece of pepperoni pizza that contained a hazy image of Jesus. "I am sure I don't have to tell you how fortunate you are to visit Augustine Manor and have the esteemed Madame Augustine take time away from her very busy schedule to speak to us."

The two dozen other agents on the bus buzzed with excitement at the potential sighting of the grand dame of the mansion. One gentleman in a bolero and boots whipped out his handkerchief to offer it to Neigh to daub unshed tears.

"Finally." Mrs. Wallis impatiently ground out while disembarking the bus. "Baby girl, that Courtneigh was just about to find one of my business cards down her throat if she didn't quit going on like Mavis Augustine was the end all, be all of the world. We're gonna ditch this party bus as soon as possible."

Sabine mouthed a big thank you. The agent tour wound its way past exquisite gardens full of dozens of dormant flower bushes including hydrangea, azalea and roses and green lawns. The massive building resembled a medieval castle complete with two turrets and a moat.

"A moat? Who puts in a moat?" Sabine peered over the rock bridge. From her vantage point, she observed two giant koi fish meandering through the moat with water flowers gracing the clear water.

Mrs. Wallis followed Sabine's gaze. "Oh dear, don't tell Micah about those fish. He'll want to come down and catch them to grill. I never understood the fascination about koi fish. You can't pet them and all they do is eat and poop. Really, of having any type of fish for that matter."

"What exactly are looking for?" Sabine continued to follow the rest of real estate sheep.

"I want to know why she's selling and why it's been on the market so long. It's been on for 18 months. But that probably is due to the widely inflated asking price. I also want to observe her since Kirby's remains found. Maybe she has scheduled the funeral and has the will."

"We are not going to traipse through this to toss an office for a will." Sabine shot back.

Mrs. Wallis looked affronted. "No, of course not. I'll create the diversion and you can search for the office. Remember: you're the one who insisted there was a crime."

Sabine gaped at her co-conspirator. She realized she had fallen for a classic Wallis Woman trap. She'd never learn.

-17-

So talented in handling male anatomy.

Life sized oil paintings of 19th century Southern aristocracy graced the ornate foyer of Augustine Manor. One particularly homely couple arrogantly stared down at the agents. Sabine had the insane urge to whip out a permanent marker and draw devil horns on the man and connecting sideburns on the woman, who was clearly a candidate for electrolysis.

Neigh caught Sabine eyeing the painting. "That's a work done by an unknown itinerant artist. The couple is Addison and Margaret Augustine. Addison's father, Montgomery Augustine, was General Stovall's best friend and one of Savannah's brave blockade runners. But Addison and Margaret are the ones who built this magnificent house. If you look to your right, you'll find an original Georgia O'Keefe as well as a face jug from Dave the Slave."

"Please follow me and we'll tour the house. On your right is the study which I believe Ms. Augustine uses as her personal office. Next to it is a powder room. Between the doors, you'll notice the one of a kind clay sculpture by the esteemed French artist Abelard Bourke titled 'Man in Rapture' which was spotlighted in *Dixie Days* last summer."

Sabine darted a look at the sculpture. She thought it was ugly in the magazine layout and it was even more unattractive in person. 'Man in Rapture' featured a naked guy holding his overly giant man part with a look of pure torture on his face. Sabine had noticed that same look on Andre, Old Lady Hughes' poodle, when he tried to mount Snookie.

Mrs. Wallis pinched Sabine's arm and inclined her head toward the office. Sabine took the hint and fell back to let Mrs. Wallis work her magic.

"Excuse me, Neigh, but could I sit for a moment and bask in this grand foyer? I'm feeling a bit overwhelmed by the sheer magnificence in the presence of this art." Mrs. Wallis swayed and pitched forward, grabbing onto the table which held the Abelard Bourke statue. When her hand landed near the delicate area of the man's anatomy, she squealed in alarm and the statue wobbled. The protruding male anatomy popped off into Neigh's outstretched hands without any prompting.

Mrs. Wallis clapped her hands together and peered at the clay penis resting in Neigh's palm. "It's a good thing you're so talented in handling male anatomy like this. Why, my Granny Lureen would have fainted dead away if she had to hold a penis in her hand. Do you have any hot glue or cornstarch? I have an old recipe for cornstarch, vinegar and corn syrup that will glue that wacker back to his proper spot."

Neigh eeked out a noise that Sabine thought sounded like a Canadian goose at war with Dingo. Then Neigh tossed the wacker high in the air near a trembling heavyset female who in turn flung it to a thin, nervous gentleman in a plaid bowtie. The flummoxed gentleman missed. The disconnected body part fell onto the Oriental rug. The entire assembly of real estate professionals scattered like an anxious flock of turkeys fleeing an angry Pilgrim at Thanksgiving. The heavier woman backed up and flopped in a red velvet chaise lounge, fanning herself into frenzied indignation and curious voyeurism. Mrs. Wallis grinned maniacally at the theatrics while Sabine attempted to stifle her giggling and fell back behind the group.

In the ensuing aftermath of the pornographic hot potato game, Sabine slipped into the office and sped over to the modern glass desk. Surrounding it were a few abstract watercolors and a triangle shaped bowl with glitter inside. *Some people have no taste,* Sabine thought to herself.

Four piles of paper littered the edge. One pile was household bills including an overdue notice for the landscape company called The Lawn Ranger. Another held receipts for gold staples at the value of $118.00. The third held paperwork concerning the cat rescue and animal practice. And the last one was where Sabine got lucky. The several dozen pages of the last will and testament of Kirby Morgan dated two years ago listed a bevy of businesses. Itching to read it, she knew she'd not have the time.

Sabine could hear the pandemonium dying down so she snapped pictures of various pages of the will and copies of other files. She barely put her phone away when a cold voice echoed from the door.

"Miss, why are you in this room?"

Sabine started when she found herself staring at the heavily Botoxed face on an overly tanned body. Madame Skank, no doubt.

"I'm sorry." Sabine apologized. "I noticed when I flushed the powder room toilet that I caught of whiff of septic backup and followed it in here. Is the house on septic or sewer? If it's septic, when was the last time the tank was pumped?"

Mavis Augustine sniffed. "I don't smell anything. But that doesn't answer my question, why are you here?"

With as many nose jobs you've had, it's a wonder you can smell at all, Sabine thought snarkily to herself. "Well, that's the problem. Your nose gets acclimated to smells and you just don't notice until you walk into a room and step in poo. I recommend your septic tank get pumped. I'm one of the agents for Katie Scarlett O'Hara Catnip Bus for Mansions." Sabine mentally hit herself and wondered if she could butcher the name any worse.

"I'll take it under advisement. Now if you please, rejoin the others in the tour." Mavis waved her orange arm toward the door. "I have to call a restorer because there's been an incident with one of my priceless works of art."

Sabine scurried by and caught up to Mrs. Wallis who had an expectant look on her face. Sabine slowly nodded and both plastered a look of awe on their faces while being led through the butler's pantry and state of the art kitchen where, according to Neigh, any maid or cook would be elated to slave away in such fine surroundings.

"Above the garage are two efficiency apartments currently being used for the live-in gardener and housekeeper." Neigh showed no signs of losing her enthusiasm. Sabine wondered how one could bounce back like that after catching a dismembered penis but Neigh somehow managed it.

The group halted at the conservatory after finishing the tour. Talking ceased at the sight of Mavis Augustine's orange body standing in the doorway.

"Do we genuflect?" Sabine leaned into Mrs. Wallis. "Do we have to kiss her ring?"

"I don't know, baby girl, but there's no way I'm going near that woman. Her fake tan will rub off onto any clothing and it's a bear to get out. She really is a skanky looking woman." Mrs. Wallis replied as Neigh ushered the group into the room. "Just a few more minutes and I'll call an Uber driver to get us back to my car."

"Welcome to Augustine Manor. I'm Mavis Augustine. Just to save everyone trouble, I have decided to take the house off the market. Call me selfish, but letting this house, this monument to history, be placed in the hands of Yankees -- or worse -- someone from Outside the Perimeter." Mavis tossed her bottle blonde shoulder length hair. "If Ms. La Fey could direct you toward the bus..."

Sabine almost felt sorry for Neigh. The junior real estate agent's shoulders drooped like she was just told her plastic surgeon cancelled her elective rhinoplasty. Mavis strolled across the room and daintily sat on one end of an elegant sofa with satin pillows while a few of the other real estate agents sniffled with sadness.

Neigh broke the silence. "Thank you, Mrs. Augustine for your inspirational speech. I totally understand." She conducted her band of followers toward the front door. "In your folders, you'll find the particulars of the other homes and their prices on our tour.

“We have a penthouse that was once reputedly owned by the inventor of the Over the Shoulder Boulder Holder bra line. And it's a bargain at $1.5 and has been totally renovated. Crass, I know, to bring up money or inspections when dealing with this jewel, but the bourgeois class insists upon it." Neigh glanced at her watch. "Would you look at the time? We'll need to be going."

"We were supposed to be able to ask questions." Sabine protested.

Mavis squinted and then frowned when she recognized Sabine. "I don't know why you want to since the house is off the market but just in an overabundance of caution, my housekeeper and the gardener tell me that we are on sewer. Septic tank is reserved for homes OTP, outside the perimeter for those who don't know. Houses outside of the 285 loop with septic tanks are made for the bourgeoisie and cost under the paltry amount of a half a million. Something a total middle-class catering agent should know."

"That's not the question I was going to ask." Sabine said innocently. "I thought you were married and your last name is Morgan. Have you planned a funeral so my associate and I can pay our respects?"

When Ms. Augustine's countenance turned an unpleasant shade the color of Pepto Bismal, Sabine continued. "I would also like to see where I can drop off my venison meatballs with the streak o' lean grits for the wake."

***

"That was one entertaining situation." Mrs. Wallis crowed. They settled in an Uber car back seat while an angry Mavis glared at them from the open front door. "You'd set the annual Metro Atlanta Real Estate Conference Christmas soiree afire if you came with me. And the streak o'lean grits? Sheer genius! I thought her orange spray tan was gonna catch fire. Did you notice the vein beside her eye? That woman ain't never eaten fatback in her life. I should have said I'd add the white dirt to the meatballs."

Sabine sniggled. Mrs. Wallis was a firm believer in adding Southern white dirt, more commonly known as kaolin, to foods to help with bathroom regularity. "That would have caused a stroke. I don't know what she was ticked off at—the fact her husband's bones were found or the threat of adding salt pork to her food. 'I'm a fruitarian' she says. When Kirby open up a meat farm, I bet she peed mango juice." Sabine plucked her phone from her purse. "Speaking of her late hubby, I got some pictures of Kirby's will."

"I'll bet a dime to a donut that she gets everything. That's why she took that pretentious fortress off the market." Mrs. Wallis shook her head. "It could have been a lovely home. Who puts that much thought and money into interior design only to make it look like highfaluting brothel!"

"And that statue figure? I wonder if the value goes down when they repair especially down there." Sabine chortled.

"That Georgia O'Keefe and jug were all copies. And that statue would be worth more if it was the real McCoy and if they found the little wacker!" Mrs. Wallis held up the piece. "Neigh and her herd of property hyenas left this on the floor. We just emasculated him—a poor copy of a bad statue." She rolled down the window of the Uber car and threw the fake Man in Rapture's penis into the streets of Atlanta. A grin began a slow crawl across her face that turned into a snicker at the thought of how she was not the first southern woman to toss a penis out a moving car.

-18-

A sales circular for Palmer's Drugs Miracle Hemorrhoid Cream.

"No, Newt. I'm not telling you how to do your job but..." Sabine tried to calm an agitated Newt. Mrs. Wallis was navigating traffic on their trek back to Jaemore County or OTP as Mavis put it. "I didn't know if you knew Mavis had been in a financial pinch. When I glanced at Mavis' paperwork on her desk in her private study, I found out she's drowning in debt. Our guide today said the gardener lives above the garage. But I saw an overdue bill from a landscaping company for quite a lot of money. And Mrs. Wallis said a lot of her art is fake. I bet she was selling her house because she needed money." Sabine quieted for a minute. "Okay. I'll see tonight. I'm grilling chicken and potatoes."

Sabine's mood became pensive. She stared out the passenger window and tried to not focus on the tone in Newt's voice.

"Baby girl, what's up? You did good today." Mrs. Wallis complimented. "I doubt Mia could have done better."

"I don't know." Sabine hedged. "Newt tried to talk to Hamilton Bilbo about the divorce but that snake oil salesman claimed he doesn't do wills and said he didn't remember anything about a divorce petition or defamation case. He said all of his older cases were in an offsite storage. When Newt asked him about the location of the storage unit, Bilbo said a former secretary forgot to pay the bill and the storage unit went up for auction. Someone really needs to call the Georgia Bar Association and complain. Maybe he'd lose his practice. Where did he go to law school? The Mail Order Law College of North Korea?"

Mrs. Wallis nodded. "I wish. But did I ever tell you that Bilbo almost got his license to practice revoked. Rumor was that he had an affair with a recent, wealthy widow from Gwinnett County named Myrtle Mansfield about twenty years ago. Her hubby, Buddy, who made a fortune with producing custom-made pasties for movie stars, was stupid enough to go to Bilbo for his will. But little old Bilbo forgot that Myrtle's brother was a probate judge somewhere in South Georgia. Big brother got wind of it and threatened to pull Bilbo's license to practice."

Sabine filed that information away for future reference and returned to her train of thought. "I've got lots of little threads trying to connect together and now Newt's kind of mad and Mia is mad at me. Everyone's mad."

"I don't know what is up with Mia. It's got something to do with Lee and a letter he got from the city of Chicago."

"What? How do you know about a letter?"

"Because the postmaster is Earl Winkie," she said, as if Sabine should know the rest.

"Oh what the heck? We're stuck in traffic for a few hours. What's the story with Earl Winkie?"

"I went to school with Earl's son, Blaise. Blaise was on the track team and his nickname was Blinkie."

"Because he was a fast runner."

"No. Where'd you get that? He tried to set the world record for longest time between eye blinks.

"But I found out that Carl Lyons—one of MeeMaw and PawPaw's kids—was going to sabotage his attempt and throw salt at Blinkie. Huckleberry, who is Carl's twin, never got along with Carl but Huck and I were always friends. We froze Mentos in ice cubes and put them in a Coke for Carl. After a few seconds, the ice melted, the Coke exploded all over Carl and he had to go home because he was covered in Coke and melted Mentos. Then Carl up and married one of the McCall sisters. You know Lottie's aunts.

Because of that, Mr. Winkie always liked me even though Blinkie developed an eye twitch during the record setting and never won. When Mr. Winkie was sorting mail, he saw the letter and told me." Mrs.

Wallis weaved her car through the traffic to merge toward the next exit.

"Is Lee moving?" Sabine couldn't imagine Lee would ever break up with Mia. One minute with them would convince the nastiest cynic that Lee adored his girlfriend.

Just then, Bruno Mars' "Uptown Funk" marched through the air. "Yes, Mia." Mrs. Wallis answered the incoming call using the car's blue tooth. "Before I forget, can you call your father and tell I'll be home in an hour. There's a chicken salad in the fridge. I can't get into another diatribe with him on why it should be against the law to give poodles foreign names. Has he been on that tirade with you? Is that what's got you all sniffly?"

"It's not that." Mia sniffed into the phone. She paused and took a deep breath. Despite the attempt to control her emotions her voice shook. "I found a letter at Lee's house a few days ago...the Chicago Fire Department offered him a battalion chief position. And it pays double!"

Mrs. Wallis glanced at Sabine knowingly. This had been exactly what Mrs. Wallis had been referring. "Mia, the question is, did he take the job?"

"I asked on Wednesday and he got mad at me for opening his mail! I didn't do it on purpose. I mean, it was just tossed on his coffee table like it was a sales circular for Palmer's Drugs Miracle Hemorrhoid Cream. We haven't talked since. He hates me! And I deserve it!" Mia let out a full fledge wail.

"He'll calm down." Sabine tried to sound soothing and reassuring to her best friend. "Did you apologize?"

"Yes, I did. I don't know what to do! He hasn't called at all." Mia whimpered and let another burst of sobs fill the dead space of the conversation.

Sabine was astounded. This was a new problem. Usually Mia was never in this position. Guys fell all over themselves trying to impress her. "Give him a few days and if he doesn't call, go to 7-11 and get him a cherry Icee."

"Maybe." Mia blew her nose into the phone. "I have to go. There's a new abuse referral that I just got assigned. Oh, Momma, Dad passed his crime scene tech. Dr. Davis, the principal at Jaemore Elementary, was his proctor. His essay was scored at a 78 since he wrote it was justifiable homicide if Old Lady Hughes touched his flags again."

"Okay. Be careful on your investigation." When the connection was broken, Mrs. Wallis could help but grin broadly. "Mia's in a hissy fit because she loves that guy. It will do her good to be at the suffering end of a relationship for a bit. She was had the upper hand in every relationship she's had, including her father. I'm not worried. Lee Kingsley loves her and he's a good guy."

"Lee told me he fell in love when she brought food over while he had poison ivy." Sabine confided. "She rubbed Granny Lureen's Crap Medicine on the rashes and the next day she was singing."

Mrs. Wallis winced at the unpleasant memory of her daughter singing. As she often said, Mia was no Beyoncé. "Besides Lee bought the old Dupont Estate last spring. It's got six bedrooms and it's on four acres. He is staying and raising a family."

There was quiet while the traffic bumped along. Sabine was able to enlarge the will on her phone. Sadly, most of the words and bottom half of the last page were illegible but Sabine could make out several of Kirby's business interests including three well known five-star hotels in New York City, Quebec and Washington D.C. Kirby had his hand in a few Michelin three-star restaurants. In addition, Kirby was sole owner of Myrrdin Natural Purlieu with an international presence in London, Paris and Milan as well as in a dozen American cities.

"I had no idea Kirby Morgan was worth this much." Sabine exclaimed. "And what in the Sam Hill is a purlieu? Have you heard of Myrrdin Natural Purlieu?"

"Goodness Sabine, you do need to get out more. Purlieu means the space surrounding an area. Like the garden in your yard is your house's purlieu. Myrrdin Purlieu is the world's most exclusive spa. All those Hollywood stars go there after wrapping up a movie to recover. Regular old people can't buy their shampoos or even get an appointment without a recommendation from your banker."

"Well, if Mavis inherits, she doesn't need to worry about money anymore so she's got several million different motives." Sabine concluded. "Now she doesn't have to sell her house and she can pay of the Lawn Ranger for all that landscaping. Too bad she won't eat streak o'lean now since she can afford it."

-19-

Lured away by the sight of a fast dwindling donut supply.

The rest of the week passed in a haze of housekeeping and writing for the local newspaper. Mia was in incommunicado mode and had not surfaced from her bedroom once she got home from work except to take a big bowl of potlikker and cornbread back to her room. Of course, Sabine had to ask what potlikker was and Mrs. Wallis informed her that it was juice left behind after boiling turnip greens, bacon and onions together. Apparently potlikker and cornbread was Mia's go-to comfort food ever since she was suspended from elementary school. Mia squeezed school glue into Lottie McCall's hair in fourth grade in retaliation for spreading the rumor that Mia's shoes were cheap designer knockoffs. Mia was also investigating convents and religious orders as a backup plan.

Sabine was able to expand on the Kirby Morgan story with carefully edited back history and the businesses he owned, or rather, his widow now owned. The newspaper should be happy to run what really constituted as news rather what Chet Chat had to say about the new Parisian fashions that were poorly copied by Janetta's Formals and Tuxedoes of Greenleaf.

Sunday dawned much cooler. It was the first time in months the temperature dipped below 50 degrees. Relief flooded Sabine. Though she could handle high temperatures after living in Texas most of her life, there were always numerous trips to Galveston Island near her hometown of Houston. Jaemore County could not boast of beaches and only offered the murky and sketchy depths of Winkie Park's pond.

Sabine drove to Athens to attend 10:00 a.m. Mass at the only Catholic church within twenty miles of her. However, try as she might, her mind drifted during the processional hymn when the melody reminded her of "Bohemian Rhapsody" by Queen and it never returned to focus on the mass.

An hour later and having no memory of receiving Communion or the homily message, Sabine wove her way to the parish hall to grab a Krispy Kreme donut and a cup of a hot liquid the hospitality committee called coffee. She was in mid bite of a glorious chocolate covered donut with cream filling when she spied Matt and Maxi Master in a deep conversation with an elderly couple. Matt, a lean giant with salt and pepper hair, towered over his petite blonde curvy wife. Sabine stuffed the rest of the donut in her mouth and casually strolled toward their location. She developed an intense interest in a three-week-old bulletin while waiting for an opening to barge her way into the conversation. Apparently, the elderly man was trying to start a mission parish for the Jaemore County community and was pitching the idea of a mission parish in Greenleaf or Hooks County to the couple. The Masters seemed amenable to a closer faith community and enthusiastically rallied for a new St. Bibana.

While she waited, Sabine pulled up St. Bibiana on her phone only to discover the 4th century martyr was the patron saint of hangovers. That would be a great patron saint for Jaemore County, she thought and then pounced when the elderly couple wobbled off, no doubt lured away by the sight of a fast dwindling donut supply.

"Mr. Master? Mrs. Master? I'm Sabine Metzke. I live in Jaemore County too and I've been meaning to come over here and introduce myself but never got around doing it."

Matthew Master flashed a grin. "You came into the Pad last week to talk to Edweener. Sorry I wasn't so friendly. I was watching a rerun of Kyle Busch going neck and neck with another car during the race." He said without a bit of remorse. "NASCAR. That's my addiction. I even watch videos to critique the drivers' techniques."

"Oh, pooh. Pay no attention to his rudeness. Call us Maxi and Matt." Maxi Master stuck out her hand

and clasped Sabine's in an iron grip. Sabine almost fell to her knees in pain.

"Maxi, hon, you're breaking Sabine's hand. Lighten up."

Maxi blasted a megawatt smile. "Sorry. One of the prizes of working as a jack of all trades in the contracting business is getting all muscle-y in places girls shouldn't."

"You're the Handy Girl?"

"Yep. And a certified public accountant, too. Although between me, you and my jolly old giant here, I am thinking about retiring that part of the business. There's only so much fake donations one can deduct for a client. Actually, the clients themselves drive me crazy. I mean how can someone who owns half of the county get pissed at me because her assistant with a hair like a bamboo forest lost a $5 tax donation form." Maxi paused for a breath. "Not that it happened in our sweet little county."

"Maxi, sweetheart, rein in that temper of yours." Matt admonished gently. "Remember what happened to that client. She's been through a lot." It was clear Matt was the peacemaker of the family.

"Pfft." Maxi waved her hand in the wind. "I can't stand snooty people. Anyway, Sabine, if you ever need a handy gal, here's my card. I do it all—plumbing, contracting, electrician, pest control, and some remodeling."

The pink business card featured a silhouette of a Marilyn Monroe type figure holding a hammer. "Any landscaping? My late aunt and uncle planted the most gorgeous yard but I didn't inherit their green thumbs."

"Not really. I tried a few years ago but I just don't have the patience. Now give me a nest of raccoons stuck in your wall and those critters will be gone within an hour. Or if you want to redo your bathroom to make it a spa, call me."

Sabine started to say goodbye but instead tilted her head. "Did you ever work for Kirby Morgan?"

"The weird animal guy?"

"Was he weird?" Sabine asked. "I heard that he actually wasn't too bad."

"No, hon, his animals were weird. Stinky bison, spitting camels, dumb ostriches, and one animal I had to look up — a yak. Did you know he was also trying to start a petting zoo and was investigating racing yaks? Crazy talk! Like who is going to bet on a yak when up against a thoroughbred horse? There is no way the Kentucky Derby people will allow a yak at Churchill Downs!"

Matt sighed again. "Maxi, you're veering off subject on one of your tangents again. We discussed this. Kirby was going to race yaks against one another at the farm and not horses. Sabine wanted to know if you worked for him."

"Oh, me and my zigzag brain! I swear. I can't remember what color underwear I have on or even if I'm wearing bloomers!" Maxi snorted and whooped loudly. Several parishioners including the priest gawked at her but Maxi paid them no attention. "He called me the day before he had that dispute with Mr. Wallis and PawPaw Lyons.

He had been excavating an area to build a bigger barn and found the remains of an old cellar. Well, honeybees—mean little bugs when riled—built nests in the old timber. He called me in a tizzy and wanted them vaporized. Said he had too many pests to take care of and since he had an ass to deal with, I could handle the bugs. I went in the next day before sunrise, met with his assistant for a half hour and killed them. It was a hard job. They had been riled up and I couldn't use the all-natural mint spray. I had to pull out the whole kit and caboodle from my protective clothing to the nasty pesticide."

Sabine was intrigued. "Before sunrise?"

Maxi nodded emphatically. "They are not active at night and they don't see too well. They get sluggish in cool night air."

"And you sent your bill to Kirby's office?" Sabine inquired.

"Yep and got paid the next week."

"By check?"

Maxi shrugged her shoulders. "I don't remember but I can look it up. Give me your phone number and email and I'll let you know." She faced her very patient husband. "Now Matt, grab me that last donut and get fueled up. We have lots to do before I jump your bones this afternoon." She cackled when she spied the shocked look on one of the super-centenarians. "Sorry Mrs. Weatherby but maybe if you let anyone get to second base with you, you'd stretch your muscles and might not need that walker!"

-20-

Being the opportunistic little...animal...she is, she drank it.

Sabine arrived home to witness Dingo lapping up Newt's coffee on an end table. Newt was absent but Sabine detected his rumbling voice outside. She flicked the curtain to watch Newt talking nonsense to one of the donkeys. Dingo, finished with the potent brew, flayed her front legs in jealousy and began a barking tirade. She followed it with what Sabine named a "derby." Dingo raced from one end of the house to another, resting a few seconds and started another lap. Newt narrowed in on the window and grinned.

Sabine's insides turned to mush. She didn't know what the future held for her and Newt but the present was pretty darn good.

"Hello *Sötnos*! " Newt kissed her forehead. "I was just telling the donkeys goodbye."

"Jenny and what's his name are going?" Sabine asked gleefully. Sabine had to close the dog door to the back yard. Dingo had not been able to do her usual patrols since she tended to herd anything with legs into submission and slavery.

"Ostie told Edweener they had no room for two donkeys at their house and gave them back to the Lyons. June Bug and Melvin Thompson are on their way." Newt reached for his coffee and frowned when he realized the mug was empty. "I must be going crazy. I could have sworn I had a full cup of coffee. Did you drink it?"

"No, that would be your canine princess." Sabine jerked her thumb toward the hallway where the blue merle stampeded into the kitchen and then collided into the back door. "She's pumped full of caffeine and nowhere to burn it off."

"Och. That sneaky girl! I should have been more attentive. No wonder she has to resort to tricks to gain attention." Newt whistled for Dingo who promptly rolled over on her back for a belly rub.

"Again, she's the dog. The coffee was in reach and being the opportunistic little...animal...she is, she drank it."

The ding of her cell phone signaled a new text. It was from Maxi Master.

Sabine,

Finished playing already and found the check. Sending a scan to your email.

Maxi

Sabine powered up her laptop and downloaded her email. There were several to attend to before she opened Maxi's. Helen Stanley assigned her two stories for the next month's edition of Dixie Days. One would necessitate a visit to Augusta to visit an expert on the care of golf courses including the prestigious Augusta National Golf Club, home of the Masters Tournament. The other was an article to document the success of the William Harris Homestead in Monroe, Georgia. The homestead was an extremely accurate restoration of a typical southern farm complete with a well-maintained family cemetery. Sabine immediately recalled Kirby's list that mentioned visiting the homestead. She filed it away in one of the cobwebs of her brain.

Her sister wanted to confirm that Newt was indeed visiting with her at Christmas. She also added that Newt would be bunking with her younger brothers, Archie and Steve, more commonly known as Steve the Meathead. Sabine blanched for a few reasons. One was her family's not so passive-aggressive message of disapproval of their living together. Second, those two male siblings were the responsible parties for calling her S & M, a horrible shortened nickname from her full name, Sabine Anne Metzke. God knows what evil machinations they were cooking up for her visit. She hoped Newt would leave all weapons in Georgia. Sabine also made a mental note to stock up on water guns and rubber bands in the event a war was declared after Midnight Mass.

She disregarded the email from the Nigerian banker who promised her $6.7 million dollars if she replied with her bank account number as well as the email ad that offered tips on how to grow a larger penis. She found Maxi's email among the cluttered inbox and clicked on it. The scan of Kirby's check for payment of ridding the cellar of the honey bees was attached.

"I'm in the wrong business." Sabine murmured. Three hundred dollars to eradicate four swarms of honey bees for a morning's work. Sabine studied the check and then the will on her phone. She kicked herself for not getting a picture of the signatures on the bottom page. She then brightened. She had snapped a picture of Kirby's writing from the to-do list.

On a hunch, Sabine printed the check and Kirby's to-do list. Grabbing her magnifying glass, she'd show them to Newt who was still pacifying Dingo by rubbing her ears and singing Swedish lullabies to the Aussie.

"I don't mean to impede your bonding but take a look. This is the check dated one week after Kirby was last seen and this is the to-do list I found in the trailer. The to-do list is from the from two years ago. The handwriting doesn't match."

Newt halted the belly rub and Dingo gave Sabine the stink eye before the Aussie slunk off to the backyard to hunt for an encroaching army of squirrels. "You're right. The 'K' in the check is much more...how do you say...curlier? But the bigger question is how do you know your to-do list was in Kirby's handwriting?"

Sabine deliberately ignored the last question and studied the check's signature more. "It's more feminine. I'd bet Mavis Augustine forged it and she knows what really happened to Kirby!" Sabine paced the living room while Newt examined both. "Can't you do anything now?" She halted and pointed to the papers.

"My first question is beside why you have a magnifying glass, is this: If Mavis did the something, why wait two years for a body that may or may not have been discovered by a compulsive digging dachshund? She could have reported him missing or even begun divorce proceedings. Any defense attorney will poke holes in this. And I still want to know how you snaked a photo of the will." Newt closed his hand over Sabine's when Sabine grimaced. "This is a great piece of evidence and I will follow-up. But please stay out of Atlanta and Mavis Augustine's way. If she is complicit in the death of her hubby, she won't think twice about hurting or even killing you."

Newt cocked his ear. "I hear a trailer. Let's get rid of the donkeys and get a cherry Icee at the 7-11. I think we deserve it and I know Dingo does after putting up with two donkeys in her yard."

***

"Fancy meeting y'all here!" A beaming Maxi Master greeted them. She was lugging the convenience store's entire inventory of Milky Ways and Snickers in a small shopping basket. "Did you get my email?"

Sabine nodded and stretched her hand out to catch an errant Milky Way from Maxi before it dropped on the floor. "Yes, thanks for sending it." She scanned the store's interior in an attempt to locate Newt. He was on the opposite side near the

Icee machines. "Did you notice anything weird about the signature on the check? It's awfully feminine."

"Oh, it was probably Mavis signing. She may have been an authorized signer on the business. I was just happy I got paid so promptly." Maxi had no idea that she had burst Sabine's bubble.

"Yeah, that makes sense. Listen, I have to go since Newt's at the register. Thanks for looking into that check." Sabine tried to sound cheery but her spirits were deflated.

"I should be thanking you! While I was going through all the paperwork for the animal farm, I realized that there was one bill I neglected to send in to 'Lanta. I did some remodeling for Kirby at his trailer here a week before he left and the amount was over $500. If I can get Mavis to pay, Matt and I can spend a long weekend at Biltmore House."

Newt handed Sabine's cherry Icee to her. "What kind of remodeling?" Newt asked.

"Some bathroom work and some rewiring." Maxi replied as she headed toward the cashier with her collection of chocolate. "Nothing major but I thought his choice of bathtub was strange."

"How so?" Sabine felt the poke of her intuition in her stomach and Newt's finger in her rib cage.

Maxi dumped her candy bars onto the counter and pointed to the clerk. "I'm not done. I see some Junior Mints I want." She turned to Sabine. "Kirby had me install the tub but the strange thing was the bathtub was one of those frou-frou ones. It had whirlpool motion, bubble making and some other stuff but Kirby didn't want me to hook it up. Just make sure it had the plumbing flowed for showers.

He had been excavating for the new barn and he wanted to be able to clean up but didn't need all the bells and whistles. He was always in a hurry."

"Yeah. Who wants to drive into Atlanta wearing dirty clothes?" Newt commiserated. Of all the difficulties in moving from Sweden, the heat was the biggest problem—a problem to which he still had some trouble acclimating.

"No, I'm pretty sure he was living at the trailer. One of the two bedrooms had a hide-away bed and he had all his clothes hanging in the closet. I know because I built in some closet shelves and a mini dresser. When I finished the tub installation, Kirby was cooking dinner and I don't mean calling for pizza or nuking a frozen meal. He was going all out. Charlotte McCall was out there, trying to fling her hair over her shoulder like she was a model. It got caught in the Craftsman radial arm saw Kirby had near the couch. We had to cut some of her hair off to get her free. I don't know about y'all but when I saw a kitchen better stocked than mine, it was apparent that Kirby had moved to the trailer and started dating Charlotte McCall."

Maxi spotted a young toddler making a grab for the Junior Mints. "Gotta go and save my Junior Mints. See ya." With that, Maxi slid aggressively between the child and her beloved Junior Mints.

"I want to go with you when you talk to Mavis." Sabine declared while buckling her seatbelt in Newt's Crown Vic cruiser. " Do you think I could be the 'bad cop'?"

"No. No. No. To answer all of your questions. She's not a suspect yet. I've already called her to see if she can come down and claim Kirby's belongings from the trailer since she is next of kin. I didn't want her to be alerted that this is a fishing expedition. She's coming in tomorrow at an 'ungodly hour.' And if I'm able, I'm going to also set aside a time to talk to Lottie."

"If Maxi is right, their marriage was on the rocks two years ago. This goes along with the divorce paperwork Edweener showed us. She offed him." Sabine leaned back and tool a long draw on her Icee.

"Offed him? Who are you? Lenny Briscoe? Columbo?" Newt heaved a sigh. "I'll let you sit behind the mirror if you promise to behave. And I mean no screaming, no pounding, no spitting, no throwing food or cans. No slashing her tires or blowing up condoms to put on her car or anything. She should not be able to even know you're there."

"Cross my heart!" Sabine accepted the limitations a little too fast.

Newt eyed her suspiciously. "You can't hire anyone to do anything remotely juvenile or illegal. And Mia can't either. In fact, no one can. No hiring some hitman or other criminal on Craigslist or on Facebook."

"Wow, party pooper. I have to tell you that this moral streak of yours takes some getting

used to, Newt." Sabine muttered.

-21-

From hauling donkeys to finding boats in trees and getting my mom's ring from Atlanta.

The next Monday found Sabine barging into Lee Kingsley's chief's office at the Jaemore County Fire Department. Lee looked up from his computer and grinned.

Sabine had noticed his blinding smile at their first meeting last April during a missing child search. Lee had also fallen hard for Mia at the same time. And though Sabine was sure Lee and Mia were deeply in love, they still had to overcome a few hurdles.

One being the height difference. Mia was a shade under six feet and Lee barely managed to make the 5'7" height requirement for the JCFD. Lottie McCall had a field day with short people jokes but Lee bore it all with grace.

The last problem was the fact that Lee Kingsley was a proud graduate of Georgia Tech. It had taken some tough love on Sabine's part for Mia, the University of Georgia alumni, to disregard a deep-seated hatred of the cross-state rivals.

"I know Mia screwed up and read your mail. She has been holed up in her room all week, missing the UGA football game on Saturday and a Flash sale at Sephora on Sunday. Just forgive her already and get over your anger." Sabine's tone broke no argument.

Lee held his hands up in surrender. "I'm not mad. And quite honestly, I've already forgotten about it. This has been such a week from hauling donkeys to finding boats in trees and getting my mom's ring from Atlanta." Lee slapped his hands over his mouth.

Sabine's ears perked up like a hound after a wounded quail. "Ring? What ring?"

"You were not supposed to hear that. Forget I said that." Lee pulled himself up and shut his office door. "Do you think you can identify that boat for me? Or even buy it maybe."

"Quit changing the subject. What ring?"

"I'm going over to The Store at lunch with the Wallis'. I was going to ask Mr. Wallis for permission to marry Mia." Lee darted his eyes around the office as if expecting to find eavesdropping equipment.

Sabine hooted in joy and then sobered. "Mia thinks you're moving to Chicago and hates her guts. I'm no Dr. Phil but that might put a snag in your plans."

"Why does she think I'm mad at her?" Lee seemed genuinely clueless.

"Duh, you've not called her or gone over to her house to talk. She's even talking about becoming a nun." Sabine closed her eyes and wondered how the human race managed to procreate at all.

"But I texted her! See here it is." Lee pressed a few buttons and there was text message dated last Friday telling Mia he was going to visit his parents in Decatur and would be back Monday morning. He even managed to slip in a few of the lovey-dovey emojis.

"But, Lee, look...it didn't send." Sabine said as she pointed out the failed message alert.

"Oh, crap in a can. Okay. You go over to Mia's office and make sure she's at Winkie Park at sundown in a bench on the far side of the parking lot. But be careful, there's Canadian goose poop on some of them because Mia will go ballistic if she's sits near it."

An hour later Sabine was banging on Mia's bedroom door in her parent's house. It was 10:00 a.m. and Mia was still barricaded in her room. Outside Old Lady Hughes was screeching obscenities at Mr. Wallis for his daily tribute to POWs. Her poodle, Andre, was woofing quietly beside the flagpoles while Snookie ran in circles in an attempt to escalate the conflict to full out war. Mrs. Wallis was already at her office, no doubt concocting some fantastic deals on unsuspecting newcomers to the area.

"I am not going away. I have my laptop, a cold twelve pack of Diet Dr. Pepper and a pizza scheduled to be delivered at 12:00." Sabine howled through the locked door. When Mia refused to answer, Sabine crossed her legs and plopped on the floor. She proceeded to boot up her laptop and fell asleep.

"Hey." Mia kicked at Sabine's hand. "You're drooling on the carpet and snoring."

Sabine started and woke herself. "If you had opened your door like an adult, there would be no drool to clean up."

"Did you say pizza?"

"I knew you could resist pizza for long." Sabine said smugly. "You just had to finish your pouting and show up."

"I wasn't pouting. I was regrouping." Mia retorted. She tossed her hair back imperiously.

"Regrouping would sound better if you were not wearing Scooby Doo pajamas and rabbit house shoes. And little lip gloss would not be a bad idea." Sabine grimaced as she stood up. A quick glance at her watch told her the pizza was due any minute. "What are you doing tonight?"

A deafening mixture of a barking Snookie, a howling Andre the Poodle blended together with Old Lady Hughes' shrill voice shattered the calm. "I don't know. What do you want to do?" Mia shrugged as she marched to the melee outside.

Sabine didn't get the chance to answer. When Mia flung open the front door, Andre slid across the wood floor into the open fireplace. Snookie followed at a frenetic pace and landed on top of the poodle.

"Amelia Juniper Wallis!" Old Lady Hughes screeched in the open doorway. Her faded pink housecoat hung on her skeletal body while the fuzzy blue hair framed her head like the halo of a fallen angel. "Your monstrous little creature has been abusing my poor Andre! She chased him from the curb and into my hydrangea bushes and then in here! What have you got to say for that?"

"Uhm, maybe Andre needs to grow a pair?" Sabine ventured.

"You stay out of this, Sabine Metzke. Your aunt was not as a nice person everyone thinks she was. And you're just as bad always ingratiating yourself like you could ever be a native Greenleafer." Old Lady Hughes punctuated each word with a poke of her bony finger.

Sabine stood as tall as her 5'3" would let her. "I'm not ever going to claim native status. I'm a Texan, born and bred by the grace of God." She was not going to let a bitter old woman insult her heritage. "Why don't we take it outside?"

Mia thrust her body between them. "Oh my goodness! Call your dog from our fireplace and go! Get him neutered or maybe if you would let Andre get a nice piece of canine booty, that might stop him from trying to mount everything in sight including my dog who was just trying to protect herself from the unwanted advances of a... sex offending...pedophile dog. He keeps this up and he's going on the Georgia Bureau of Investigation's sex offender registry."

Old Lady Hughes turned her attention to her neighbor. "Just so you know, I'm keeping track of all the crimes this animal of yours has committed. Wait until Sally Jackson gets an exclusive interview with me about that wienie dog trying to dig up every dead person in the county including Dorcas Priest and Kirby Morgan." With that threat, she whistled for her dog and backed out of the door. Poor Andre left a wake of soot and leaves as he lumbered after his volatile mistress.

"What are you doing?" Mia asked as Sabine studied the area where Old Lady Hughes had stood.

"Looking for fire and brimstone in her wake. Maybe we can put some sort of witch trap on your floor like they do in all those demon possession movies."

"Stop it. The pizza dude is here and you still have to tell me what we're doing tonight. It's the best offer I've had since Lee broke up with me. Even my parents have deserted me in my time of need." Mia dug through her purse for tip money. Big tips were necessary as the closest pizza delivery was in nearby in Hooks County. Mia didn't want to burn that bridge. "I also want to pick your brain on how to start a new religious order. Something along the lines of the Shopping Sisters of Rodeo Drive.

"You do know most nuns take a vow of poverty, obedience and chastity? You like guys too much. You suck at listening to people who try to tell you what to do. And nuns and sisters don't wear Coach boots and Hermes perfume. Lastly, you're not even Catholic." Sabine scoffed. "Are you sure Lee broke up with you? It doesn't seem Lee's style." Sabine would have her hands full trying to convince Sister Mia of the Holy Gucci Bag to visit Winkie Park tonight. It was the spot were Lee had told her to where to go was his and Mia's make out spot for six months. If Mia thought they were kaput, then all Sabine could do was hog tie her and drag her through the duck poo to the bench.

-22-

Mindless of his dress pants alighting in poo, dirt and pond sludge

"Why are we here?" Mia stopped mid-bite into her foot-long Coney from Sonic. "You said we could eat and walk around. I thought you meant the mall."

Sabine held her hands out innocently. "To be quite honest, I never said we'd walk the mall. After visiting Sephora all afternoon, I thought maybe we could commune with nature seeing you're thinking about becoming a cloistered nun. This might be your last chance to hunt Julius Squeezer before you take your vows."

Sabine exited the Challenger before Mia could swipe the keys. "Come on. Don't be a party pooper."

"Poop is right. All these geese use this area as their own personal portable toilet." Mia dodged a few white mounds. "You had better be glad I'm wearing my running shoes. And that Julius Squeezer boa constrictor myth is something Mayor Crumbee made up to attract those reality TV crews looking for things like Bigfoot ten years ago. There is no way this park is housing a thirteen-foot snake."

"Oh. Well, let's go sit over that way. The sunset is supposed to be spectacular since the smog in Atlanta was so brutal today."

Mia frowned. "Quit lying. Smog does not affect a sunset."

Sabine jutted out her chin. "Does so. You don't know anything about stuff like that. You're not a science person. You said it yourself that you almost failed geology in college. You thought there would be semi-precious jewels to study and there would be field trips to jewelry stores."

"That was not my fault. Geology is the study of rocks. Who would've thought that dodgy Dr. Hermann didn't think it was important to know the birthstones for every month?" Mia defended herself.

Sabine searched for a goose poop free bench and found one. Mia deemed the bench was clean enough to sit down on and kept up her monologue on the teaching standards of birthstones while finishing off her limeade. Sabine surreptitiously checked her phone for any communication from Lee. The sunset was in ten minutes and she, Mia, and a few Canadian geese were the only park visitors. Sabine was getting antsy and wished for Julius Squeezer or the Chupacabra to make an appearance to pass the few minutes in lieu of Mia's blustering.

Just when the sun touched the horizon in a beautiful collection of lavender, orange, peach and yellow, a siren pierced the air. The giant hook and ladder truck peeled into the parking lot, narrowly missing Sabine's Challenger. Mia gasped in disbelief and Sabine shuddered in relief at the same time. And like a few days before, all of Jaemore County turned out to rubber neck and once again proved the scarcity of recreation resources in the area.

Lee Kingsley, resplendent in his dress uniform, flew out of the driver's side while Mr. Wallis with a grin reminiscent of the Mona Lisa on steroids popped out of the passenger seat. Mrs. Wallis clambered down looking slightly nauseous and eyes glazed over. Newt pulled up behind the truck and was beaming.

Lee floated to Mia who was looking more and more thunderstruck. He patiently waited until the entire population of Greenleaf circled behind him.

"Hey, Mia." Lee began. He shifted his feet from side to side and he fine sheen of perspiration on his forehead. It was apparent he was nervous.

"I'm mad at you, Leland Bryce Kingsley, Junior. And I believe from your lack of communication, that we are no longer an item." Mia stuck her nose in the air and deliberately twisted away from Lee.

Lee, still grinning, grabbed her knees and swiveled her back to face him. "I did text you but Sabine pointed out that that the text never sent. I went to Decatur this weekend to get something from my mother."

A suspicious sniffle echoed through the crowd. Mr. Wallis was tearing-up. Mrs. Wallis hurriedly thrust a tissue in his hands.

Finally, the incongruity of the situation dawned on Mia. "Wait, what are all y'all doing here?"

"Because." Lee bent on one knee, mindless of his dress pants alighting in poo, dirt and pond sludge. "I want to ask you something and it was the only way I could get permission from your father. Will you do me the honor of becoming my wife, Amelia Juniper Wallis?" With that, he slid his right hand out of his pocket to reveal a stunning Art Deco garnet ring in a cluster of diamonds.

Mia opened her mouth and closed it without a sound. Lee took her left hand and slid the opulent piece of jewelry onto her ring finger.

"Say something, Mia." A bystander yelled.

"Oh my God! Yes! " Mia leapt up like a Mexican jumping bean after drinking two lattes. The applause was deafening, only punctuated by a loud nose blowing courtesy of Mr. Wallis.

"Break out the shine!" Edweener's gravelly voice rose above the racket.

The crowd whooped and hollered as Alvin and the Lyons' Pride Carport Band broke out their instruments to celebrate. MeeMaw directed the setup of large cauldrons of Brunswick stew and cornbread while PawPaw silently attended to the disbursement of several gallons of sweet tea. Mr. and

Mrs. Wallis were inundated with congratulations and advice on wedding plans.

Mrs. Wallis threaded her way toward her daughter. Mia was still shell shocked. "My baby! " Mrs. Wallis enveloped her in a huge hug with one hand and grabbed Sabine in the other. "So much planning! We've got to find a dress, flowers, a date and a million other details. I already talked to Lane Camden from Spring Avenue Photographers. You know her. She did your cousin Octavia's wedding last year and did a fabulous job hiding that giant hairy mole on that maid of honor's forehead. And Lane also managed to Photoshop Octavia's belly so that she didn't look like she was in her second trimester. And to think she wore white. What photographers can do these days with computers!" Mrs. Wallis ended her speech and waited expectantly for Sabine to comment.

"Uhm, why shouldn't Lane Camden wear white?"

Mrs. Wallis shook her head. "No, Octavia wore white. Lane Camden wore a lovely Michael Kors outfit but to be honest she ruined it by wearing the wrong shoes."

"Momma!" Mia jerked herself out of her stupor

"Shoes make or break an outfit." Mrs. Wallis went on as if she didn't hear her daughter.

"Momma! If you don't stop talking about Octavia, I'm going to elope." Mia threatened.

"Well, I'll be." Mrs. Wallis huffed. "Then let's talk about Sabine's maid of honor dress. I was thinking a lovely green in a jewel tone or maybe a deep blue." Mrs. Wallis appraised Sabine's height.

"Yes. Definitely jewel tones. And Snookie will look wonderful as the ring dog."

Mrs. Wallis lowered her voice and leaned into Sabine. "Now we have an excuse to visit Myrrdin Natural Purlieu for a spa day if we book it before the wedding."

-23-

Her empty head with fake hair

It wasn't until the next morning that Sabine was able to steal a few minutes to lean back into Newt's arms on their couch watching the early morning local news, “Daybreak Atlanta”, on Channel 7. The sun had just kissed the horizon, but Dingo was still curled up at their feet, snoring. Sabine scrunched up her face when Sally Jackson, the clueless investigative reporter, swooped onto the screen.

"Stu, you may remember a few months ago when I put my life in peril to report about the raging meth problem tucked away in Jaemore County." Sally paused to fling an errant lock of hair off her shoulders and over green silky dress. The camera followed her across the studio to a background of the burnt trailer that housed a meth lab run by Lindy Mills, presently incarcerated in a South Georgia prison.

"Oh my God!" Sabine sat up and disrupted Dingo's nap. "Do you see that?"

"What? Lindy Mills' mobile drug lab?" Newt leaned in to get a better look.

"No. Sally is wearing a green dress in front of a green screen. All you see is her empty head with fake hair!"

Sure enough, the floating head of Sally Jackson complete with peroxide blonde tresses hovered over the green screen while giving a running commentary.

"Now a mere few months later, the remains of local businessman, Kirby Morgan, were found in his defunct exotic animal processing facility. You might remember about the violent digging at the final resting place of one Dorcas Priest in Greenleaf. Well, the vandals got more than they bargained for when they tried to wreck the remains of the business and dug up Mr. Morgan. Tune in today at noon for a live interview with Mavis Augustine, Mr. Morgan's beloved spouse, at her historic house in Buckhead."

The camera cut back to the anchor and Sabine had to give it to Stu for maintaining his composure while conversing with a disembodied reporter.

"What kind of babbly bullcrap is she saying?" Sabine scrunched up her nose. "Was there a vandalism report at the animal ranch?"

"Nope. She's not going to like it when I file the prelim report that a roving dachshund is the organizer and sole member of the vandals." Newt grinned. "And I might just send her to Mrs. Wallis since she is Snookie's legal guardian and sell tickets. Wonder if that is illegal?"

"The selling tickets or sending Sally over to Mrs. Wallis?"

"Either one." Newt retracted his arm from Sabine and shook dog hair from his blue jeans. "Now remember that Mavis is due at the Sheriff's office at 10 so you need to be there at 9:45ish to take your place as official busybody behind the two-way mirror."

Sabine's eyes gleamed. "I'll be there."

***

Sabine quietly popped the top on her cold Diet Dr. Pepper and carefully laid out her freshly popped popcorn and Raisinets. It would not due if she had to run out for a drink or food and miss anything.

The light in the interrogation room blinked on and Newt's eyes flickered to the two-way mirror. A heavily made up Mavis Augustine glided into the room with the smoke of a lit Virginia Slims 100 wafting toward Newt.

Mavis frowned at the utilitarian chair as if judging its' fashion less qualities. With a bigger puckered brow, she sat gingerly on the edge.

"Now, Mr. Johnson, what is it you need of me? I'm simply swamped with funeral arrangements." Mavis stuck her nose up in the air in an attempt to look down on Newt.

Newt's polite smile belied his aggravation. Sabine knew that smile all too well as he used it several times on her and Mia. "It's Detective Johansson, Ms. Morgan. We're a non-smoking facility. Could you put out your cigarette?" Newt pointed toward a coffee cup with smidgeon of water. "I just have a few questions, you know, for follow-up for the Georgia Bureau of Investigation and the US Department of Agriculture since Mr. Morgan imported nonnative animals." Newt lied smoothly. "When was the last time you saw your husband?"

After extinguishing her smoke, Mavis tried to crinkle her forehead but the heavily Botoxed skin refused to budge. "My name is Ms. Augustine. I never took my husband's name. As to your question, I would have to say it was two days after those horrible delinquents let all of poor Kirby's animals go. It was the last straw for him. The con artist who sold him that...that...wasteland refused to refund the money. This God-forsaken county just killed my partner and here you are, making me relive it." Mavis pulled out a silk handkerchief and daintily blew her nose. She placed back into her Kate Spade bag and waited expectantly for Newt to apologize.

Having lived with Sabine for a few months, Newt was not moved by Mavis' act. "But according to our records, two years ago this past September he went to the annual Chicken Daze Ball with..." Newt flipped the papers in the file as if he didn't remember. "With Charlotte McCall. So you were okay with your husband going to a dance with another woman?"

"I couldn't make it the ball. I know Kirby, bless his heart, was a prominent figure in this dinky county but we were opening the first Myrrdin Natural Purlieu in New York and I had to be there to supervise. Mr. Johnson, you have no idea the labor and supply problems one could have when opening up a haute skincare line. Why, the demands would just eat you alive. I told Kirby that I would take care of it."

"It's Detective Johansson by the way. But I don't understand why you never reported him missing. He's been gone for two years and there's nothing. We did get an inquiry the day after the ball but why didn't you call?" Newt's smile didn't reach his blue eyes.

Mavis managed to look aggrieved. "He came by the house after the day after the ball to pack for a trip to Montana or was it Edmonton? Then he was off to research more exotic livestock." She shook her head and Sabine was surprised to see a frown line on Mavis' forehead. "We got into a terrible row about how he refused to give up on that idiotic animal farm. He wanted to buy more stock and I thought he was spreading himself too thin. We had been fighting for a few months about the farm. I was in the process of becoming a fruitarian and didn't want anything to do with the slaughter of animals. I told him to never come back. I had it with his stubbornness and insensitivity to the animals' plights. Just because humans won the genetic lottery by developing thumbs doesn't mean we can impose our value and thought system on other sentient beings."

Newt cocked his head. "We found Kirby's briefcase and there was an unfiled petition for divorce as well as one for defamation. But didn't you get suspicious when your husband never came back from the trip or follow through with the divorce?"

"Mr. Johnson, clearly you didn't know Kirby. He always was a drama king. Threatening divorce was a weekly occurrence. He never was going to divorce me. I was his money and ticket into Atlanta. After all, I can date my family back to beyond the War of

Northern Aggression. I was just letting him pout and then get over it."

Mavis rummaged through her purse and retrieved her cell phone. "Now, Mr. Johnson, correct me if I'm wrong but this is sounding more and more like an interrogation. Am I suspected of something?"

"Ms. Morgan, I apologize. I'm following up on the case since the GBI is so far behind. Just a few more questions and I'll show you out. Did Mr. Morgan have a dated will?"

"No, he didn't have a will. He didn't need one. What are you implying? Kirby was my husband! I automatically inherit his businesses and money as his surviving spouse via the intestate succession clause!" Mavis' eyes popped out of their sockets as her voice raised to reveal her indignant outrage.

In the other room, Sabine was engrossed. Shoving popcorn into her mouth, she knew Hollywood could never come up with a more mesmerizing scene. What was Newt up to?

"Just to clarify. You're stating on the record, there's no will?"

At Mavis' nod, Newt continued, "But according to your previous statement, it was you who had all the money and influence due to your longstanding...shall we say, familial relationship...in the community. Then you implied that Mr. Morgan was broke."

Mavis opened and closed her mouth like a big mouth bass caught in a net.

"Yet when I checked out Mr. Morgan's businesses, all were in his name. Your name, whether you go by Mavis Morgan or Mavis

Augustine, was never on the paperwork. All his businesses are being run by people Kirby put in place before he started the Exotic Animal Farm. What I want to know is, why did you lie to me?" Newt tilted his head as if he was a lion appraising a small elk. He carefully opened a manila folder and presented a copy of the check Maxi Masters emailed to Sabine for payment of the eradication of the yellow jackets. "Also why would Mr. Morgan want to file a cease and desist order against you? And Mr. Morgan was missing for two years. Did you not wonder where he was? Even if he left for three months to stock up on inventory, that's still quite a long time to not hear from your husband."

Mavis gaped at the check copy and then popped up from her seat and flung her bag on her shoulder. "This conversation is over. If you need to talk to me again, contact my attorney, Garland Sterling of Sterling Law Offices. You can find him in Buckhead off Peachtree Street."

With that, Mavis stomped out of the interrogation room just as Sabine opened her door.

-24-

You have my penis!!

"OU!!" Mavis screamed. "I know you. You have my penis!!"

Sabine started at first and then responded back. "I have nothing of the sort. I'm perfectly fine with my hoo-haa."

Mavis snarled like an angry Chihuahua on drunk of single malt whiskey. "My Man in Rapture is missing his penis. And you were in my private study during the real estate tour complaining of septic backwash." Mavis' right index finger jabbed Sabine on her chest. "And now you're here. You're the reason behind this."

Undeterred, Sabine stepped forward and smelled the choking scent of a heavy application of perfume wafting from Mavis. "Touch me again and you'll be missing something more than your wacker."

Newt peered out the interrogation door, alarmed to find a suspect and his girlfriend inches away from a brawl.

"Mr. Johnson, you need to arrest this woman on theft. She came into my house and stole the penis from my irreplaceable statue and irrevocably damaged it. I demand you search her for the penis." Mavis dictated imperiously.

Newt raked his hands through his thinning blond hair. "When and where did this alleged theft take place?"

"A few days ago at my house in Buckhead."

"Did this young lady break into your house?" Newt calmly asked. "And did you witness the theft of the male appendage?"

"Well." Mavis' jaw set mulishly. "No but she came under the pretext of being a real estate agent. Surely that's illegal."

Sabine could not hold back any longer. "I was considering a career change and was thinking about real estate. I was with a licensed real estate broker as an intern. And that penis came off because of a wobbly table and I was nowhere near when the statue. Lost. His. Manhood." She punctuated with a pointed finger toward Mavis. "And you, crazy lady..."

Newt pulled Sabine away from an increasingly nervous Mavis who backed away slowly. "Perhaps you need to leave. But don't leave the country. I'll have to notify the federal authorities if you do."

Mavis swiveled on her three-inch heels and clapped out of the building with an allergy inducing cloud of Chanel #5 without another word.

"So you posed as a real estate agent and emasculated a statue?" Newt frowned. He wondered if there was legal precedent to inject a GPS tracker or a time release anti-psychotic medicine patch in an adult in the state of Georgia. "Care to tell me when and how the castration exactly happened?"

Sabine bit her lip and opted for complete honesty. "I didn't break the statue. Mrs. Wallis and I hitched a ride on some psycho real estate tour in Buckhead. Mavis' mansion was the first stop. Mrs. Wallis bumped a table and off popped Man's wacker into Neigh's hands. Or was it Nay's hands? She has great reaction times. She must be a pro at drinking games like beer pong." Sabine stopped and pondered the ramifications of Neigh's reflexes. "Is there an Olympic sport that Neigh can enter?"

Newt crossed his eyes. For the life of him, he couldn't remember the original question.

Sabine shook herself and continued. "During the castration bit, I slipped into Mavis' private office. I saw overdue bills for a lawn service, stuff for her crazy cat rescue and the last few pages of Kirby's will. Only by the time I reached for it, the door was opening and I could only get a few pictures of it."

"That's when we discovered that Mavis does not have septic and she took the house off the market. She got kind of mad when I asked her about Kirby and even madder when I offered to make meatballs for the wake."

"You admit you snuck in under false pretenses and searched her office knowing her husband was dead and she might be a criminal?" Newt asked in a deceptively quiet voice.

Sabine attempted a feeble grin and tried to redirect Newt's questions. "I wasn't alone. I had Mrs. Wallis and that crazy bus of real estate hawkers. But why does she have overdue notices from a lawn company when she said she had a gardener? And why are all her works of art fake? I looked it up and in Georgia if there is no will, the surviving spouse automatically inherits everything. I bet she was on the verge of bankruptcy when Kirby disappeared and now that he's turned up as a pile of bones, she knows she gets everything if she stays quiet about the will I found on her desk. And then she took Augustine Manor off the market after it had been on for over a year. Something's hinky, Newt. I'd bet Mavis' silicone filled body on it."

The distraction worked. Newt's mind whirled with conspiracies and ideas. "We know Kirby put some people in place to run his businesses. Who was eventually going to get all that money in that will? If Mavis is hiding a will, she'll be in contempt of court. Georgia law permits a judge to issue sanctions in the form of criminal fines and jail time if the will is not delivered to the court. It'd be a misdemeanor with a fine and a small jail sentence. All we have to go on is your cell phone pictures. And that doesn't prove a thing in court. Even if Kirby was in the beginning process of divorce. The district attorney won't do anything and Mavis' attorney would shred that." Newt rubbed his chin. "I see your points but without a clear cause of death, all we have is that she failed to report him missing and even then, it just proves she was a horrible spouse. But I have to ask. Where's the broken penis?"

"Somewhere on Interstate 85 near the connector. Mrs. Wallis and I are much too ladylike to hold on a fake penis that isn't ours."

-25-

Don't forget that you already have a broom since you flew it up here.

Sabine arrived home to garbage on the floor in her kitchen and a missing Australian Shepherd. She hurriedly checked the balance in her checking account because she knew the dog would go for the money in the event of a clash with police or animal control. What little money that was in there remained.

The doggie door was open to the back yard but the fence gate was locked. It was truly a locked door mystery. Calling Dingo's name while taking the trash out was futile as well as shaking the dog treat container.

By lunchtime, Sabine started to worry. Dingo was never one to wander. The dog knew exactly where the food came from and nothing would have made her leave the house. Sabine called Newt who promised to put out an APB on the missing merle.

Unable to sit still, Sabine snatched up Dingo's leash and decided to forage around the land near her house. Across the street was a retaining pond for a defunct neighborhood development. And that was where she heard the familiar bark and snarl.

Despite the chain-link fence surrounding water, Sabine spied her Aussie near the drainage pipe. Muddy with matted hair, Dingo refused all orders to return to Sabine's side.

"You are the most God-awful animal to ever exist." Sabine muttered as she clumsily climbed the fence. She maneuvered gently through the tall grass, keeping a watchful eye for hostile animals like chipmunks and the squirrels Dingo had enraged.

Sabine seized Dingo's collar to attach the leash. "You are so in trouble for this." Sabine threatened. "Let's go."

Dingo laid down and rebuffed any attempt at movement. She even curled her paws around the grate of the drainage pipe and held on as if her last living breath depended on her canine grip.

"What is the deal?" Sabine leaned closer and became aware of a slight rustling noise and sniffing. "If this is a skunk, you'll be the adoptable dog of the month at Animal Control because you're toast."

The dead leaves parted and out popped two small kittens. Having never owned a cat in her life, Sabine couldn't discern the age but was happy to see the kittens' eyes were open. One was black with a white stripe across its' nose and the other was a calico.

"Is this why you ran? Are you that noble? Are you that noble to everyone but me?"

In response, Dingo yawned and pawed at the locked grate.

"Yeah, yeah, yeah. I get it. Call for help." Sabine whipped out her cell phone and called Lee.

Armed with four of Jaemore County's finest firefighters and hastily repurposed crow bars, the massive grate was lifted enough for the diminutive Lee to slither in to apprehend the kittens.

"Where do you want them?" Lee grasped the kittens gently as he petted the black and white one.

"Me?" Sabine stuttered. "I've never had a cat. I don't even know how to use a litter box!"

Lee extended the arm carrying the calico. "Sabine, how do you not know anything about cats? You don't use the litter box. The cats will. They're about eight weeks old. Probably ready to weaned. In a few months, they'll have to be spayed."

"Oh, no. No. No. No. Dingo will eat them alive or put them up on eBay. We can't handle more girls in the house." Against her better judgment, Sabine cuddled the calico. She was rewarded with a purr louder than her Dodge Challenger. Dingo even jumped on her hind legs and licked the kitten. The kitten responded with a return lick. "Where's the momma cat? I mean, if I was a cat, I'd be pretty ticked off to find my kittens kidnapped. Shouldn't we put up posters?"

Lee leaned in and jerked his head back toward the storm drain. "The momma cat is in there. It looks like she died a few hours ago from a tangle with a wild animal. But you're right. I'll take them to Animal Control. Hopefully, they will be adopted fast." Lee allowed his voice to trail and allowed the unsaid potential demise of the kittens to hang in the air.

Sabine ignored the thought of the unspoken words. She really didn't have the time to care for two orphan kittens.

"But Animal Control will have to put them down after a few days if they're not adopted because there is no room." Lee played the trump card by verbalizing what both of them were thinking. He studied Sabine's face, playing on her love of animals. The black and white settled contentedly in the crook of Lee's arm. "Would you hate to be responsible for innocent deaths?"

When Sabine didn't respond, he continued. "How about I take one and you take the other? My house is home to a few field mice." Lee offered when he spied the softening of Sabine's resolve by the way her body relaxed and the petting of the kitten became long, slow strokes with a few scratches in key "kitty heaven" spots.

Lee had bought a large estate built by the Duponts when he moved to Jaemore County from Atlanta. Built in 1839 by Lucas Dupont for his wife, Glenda, it had been neglected tremendously by the Dupont family until the last direct descendent died several years ago. Lee had slowly made progress and was ecstatic to remove the bat guano from the attic. Earlier this year, he had thrown a "Bueno from Guano" party on National Bat Appreciation day for the fire department personnel.

"And plus, when Mia and I get married, she'll have to leave Snookie at her mom's. Having another pet will make things easier for her."

Sabine heaved a sigh. "Okay. I'll keep this...what did you call it...comical?"

"Calico." Lee corrected. "I'll take both of them to see Dr. Emberly to get them checked and I'll drop her by Newt's office." He turned but stopped. "You did a good thing, Sabine. And you too, Dingo. It's a shame you won't have puppies of your own."

***

Sabine wove her way past Dupont's produce and healthy foods to arrive on the cookie aisle. If there was ever a need for chocolate, it was today for Sabine.

As she waffled between chocolate covered marshmallows and Oreos, she spied a fast-moving object resembling a brown patch of pampas grass in her peripheral vision at the end of the aisle. She groaned. Charlotte McCall, aka Lotta Hair, was in the building.

Remembering her manners at the last minute, Sabine smiled at Lottie when Mia's nemesis stopped in front of the ginger snaps.

"Hello, Lot...tie." Sabine bit the inside her mouth to forestall the Lotta Hair moniker. Lottie was still looking like death warmed over. Dressed in a wrinkled blue dress, Lottie's pinched face was highlighted by a poor choice of coral lipstick. Her hair managed to be oily, wiry and frizzy at the same time—a feat Sabine never thought could be found in nature.

Lottie narrowed her rodent eyes at Sabine, nodded curtly and returned to shopping.

Sabine peered over into Lottie's buggy and was astounded to find it full of cleaning supplies. Sabine was positive that Madame Matilda Greenleaf Jaemore employed a housekeeper as well as a cook and maid. That thought led to Sabine's lips before her filter could catch up.

"Why are you buying all that? Don't y'all have a maid to shop for y'all?"

Of all the responses Sabine thought Lottie would spout, sobbing in the middle of Dupont's Supermarket was not even in the top ten.

Lottie wailed as if she answering a mating call to a male elephant and slid to the floor.

Sabine whispered, "It's fine. I was just making polite conversation. I don't give a rat's butt if you have to shop for furniture polish." She leaned in and patted Lottie's back the same way she petted Dingo.

Lottie swiveled her head, almost poking out Sabine's eye with her hair. "It's not that, you...you...person." Lottie lowered her head in her hands and continued to caterwaul.

"Gee, what a great comeback." Sabine deadpanned. Sabine pondered if she should offer Lottie help or a sympathetic shoulder. "Maybe we should get you up and into your casket. I mean your car so you can get back home."

"Home? Home?" Lottie blubbered as she wiped her nose on the end of Sabine's shirt.

Sabine backed away disgusted. Would anyone notice if I shopped with only my tank top and bra straps showing, she thought? She shrugged and pulled off her shirt, making sure she didn't touch Lottie's oozy deposit.

"Yes, home. What has gotten into you?" Sabine handed Lottie the shirt to finish her mucus cleanup.

"Ms. Tilda is selling Jaemore Manor and downsizing to one of those homes where she lives." The "she" was full of loathing with an underlying thread of disgust. "The staff has been let go except for me. And now it's up to me to get the Manor ready for selling."

Sabine knew, without asking, to which 'she' Lottie was referring Mia. But that didn't answer any of the other questions that popped up from Lottie's revelation. Ms. Tilda leaving Jaemore Manor, a house that had been in her husband's family for generations? A house that survived General Sherman's March to the Sea during the Civil War? It was a widely accepted fact that Sherman was to cut through Jaemore County on his way to Savannah but at the last moment, the Union army swerved, completely avoiding what many considered the Cesspool of the South.

"Why?"

Lottie looked up at Sabine and said "And it's all your fault. If you were not at that animal farm and found Kir...Kirby's body, Ms. Tilda would have never driven out there and saw *her* neighborhood. Ms. Tilda fell in love with a single-story ranch and that's that." When she finished with her tirade, Lottie slung Sabine's shirt on the sugar wafers and stomped off with her buggy of Lysol and mops.

"Don't forget that you already have a broom since you flew it up here." Sabine called after and was rewarded with a less than lady-like hand gesture from Lottie.

Sabine made her way to the pet food aisle. "Yeah, it's a real shame 'you won't have puppies of your own'" Sabine mimicked Lee as she lugged a twenty-pound container of cat litter and a large assortment of kitten food and toys. "She just had to be noble. And I had to talk to Lottie and now I have a cat."

"Sabine, who are you talking to?" Shay Edmunds, one of MeeMaw's grandchildren, asked from behind.

"Myself. Apparently, I have adopted a calico kitten." Sabine shook her head. "Do you recommend a certain kind of kitten food?"

Shay had started working at Dupont's when her shiftless husband, Tim-Tom the Moronic Coroner, served her divorce papers after Shay gave birth to their child and was recuperating in the hospital. Surprising everyone, she quickly climbed the ladder from cashier to assistant manager in four months. She was even taking online classes for a business degree at night at Mrs. Wallis' urging.

"Technically, I supposed I should recommend the highest price one or our store brand but honestly, your run of the mill food should be good unless Dr. Emberly tells you otherwise."

A stray thought struck Sabine. "I know there are privacy rules but if I showed you a picture of a medicine, could you see whose prescription this is? I found it at the Animal Farm and I think it's Kirby Morgan's."

Shay waffled. "Gee, Sabine. I don't think I can. It's not my department and there are federal privacy laws..." She trailed off apologetically.

Sabine heaved a sigh. "I totally get it. I just want to make sure Mrs. Wallis doesn't get arrested for Kirby's murder." Sabine was not above using any emotional blackmail to achieve her gains. She knew Shay would do anything for her benefactor.

Shay perked up. "Mrs. Wallis? Why didn't you say so in the first place? You stay here and I'll be back in a few minutes." She snatched Sabine's phone and hurried over to the lanky towheaded pharmacist.

After deciding to purchase a mix of kitten food, Sabine zoomed in line, cutting off an irate Hamilton Bilbo buying a toilet plunger and anti-fungal medication.

"Well, hello. If it isn't my favorite Texas transplant." Bilbo sidled up to Sabine's buggy and inspected her selections. "Based on your groceries, I'd say you have a new pussy...cat, that is."

Sabine managed to swallow the vurp before it projected onto Bilbo's Italian suit. "Why, yes. I do have a new pet as well as a new Remington shotgun. Care to come out to be my target practice?"

"Oh, baby. You couldn't catch me on your best day." Bilbo's black eyes gleamed.

"Well, that growing bald spot that you tried unsuccessfully to comb over makes a perfect bullseye." Sabine pasted a phony smile. "You wouldn't know about Kirby Morgan's will or the divorce petition, would you?"

"I told your boyfriend that I don't do wills anymore."

"Why, Hamilton Bilbo, as I live and breathe. In my little old store." Shay sashayed over to her husband's divorce attorney. Bilbo gulped loudly as he tried to shrink into the background.

Sabine leaned back, happy to have a front row seat to another show. She knew Bilbo had propositioned Shay after the final divorce date. Half of Jaemore County plastered themselves around Judge Monroe's small courtroom. What Bilbo failed to remember was Shay was part of the Lyons clan and they didn't like cheaters nor the scum that defended them. Suffice it to say, Bilbo barely made it to his office after being pummeled with jeers, threats, and a large black rat snake snuck in under the noses of the bailiffs.

"Now, *ma cherie*." Bilbo began in a faux Italian accent. "All's fair in love and war, right?" He began to back into the impulse area full of candy bars and tabloid magazines.

"You're faking an Italian accent but talking French." Sabine marveled at his dated pickup line.

"Now, you just buy your stuff and leave. I'm a lady but I'm about to chew up nails and spit out a barbed wire fence at you."

Bilbo took Shay's threat to heart and fumbled out after paying.

"That POS makes me so...." Shay's body shook with anger. "I had hoped he would never darken Dupont's after the divorce but yet here he is."

"Uhm, did you find out anything about the prescription?" Sabine asked in an overt way to change the subject and talk Shay down from her hissy fit.

Shay jerked her head back after glaring at Bilbo's car squealing out of the parking lot. "Oh, yeah.

Tammy said it was Kirby Morgan's prescription based on the numbers and medicine."

"And Tammy is the...?"

"Pharmacist." Shay finished, blushing beet red.

"Why are you blushing?"

Shay glanced around and tilted her head to Sabine. "I like her."

Realization dawned on Sabine. "Oh, you like her."

"Yeah. And she likes me." Shay whispered. "What am I going to tell my parents?"

Sabine shrugged. "Shay, you gotta do what you gotta do. I think parents will probably say if you're in a healthy relationship with someone who treats you with respect, then they'd be okay with it."

Shay showed relief. "Thanks. But if you don't mind, don't tell anyone. I want to be sure of our feelings and I don't want Tim-Tom or Bilbo to use it against me to try to take my son away."

"Your secret is safe with me. You can always tell people that Tim-Tom was such a bad lover, you switched sides."

"I like the way you think, Sabine." Shay smiled. "And tell you what—your purchases are on me today."

-26-

It’s like Sabine’s brain is constipated.

Sabine returned home with her load of kitten supplies and walked in her house to find Newt laying on the floor, cuddled up with an overweight Australian Shepherd and a tiny calico in the crook of his arms. Her heart melted as she overheard Newt explain to Dingo how fragile a kitten was. Dingo, still in her noble maternal role, seemed to hang on every word.

“Have you got a name?” Sabine was loathed to interrupt but the weighty cat litter was cutting off her circulation in her hand.

Newt gently scratched behind the kitten’s ears while Dingo gave it a thorough bath. “I don’t know. I was thinking of Calvin because of the markings.”

“Calvin. Calvin.” Sabine let it roll off her tongue. “I like it. But you do know the kitten's a girl.”

Newt smiled. "Since when do we do things traditional? What other couple pairs smoked brisket and *raggmunk*? Or who else mixes queso dip and Walpurgis Night?"

Sabine also grinned. "I see your point. Calvin it is. We'll need to set up her litter box."

Newt laughed uproariously. "Nope. Calvin followed Dingo out the doggie door and did her business beside her canine sister. They came back in and played on your side of the bed. It was so sweet! I took a picture of them and texted it to you."

Sabine pulled up the picture and noticed Dingo and Calvin did indeed mug it up for the camera with an action shot of both licking her pillow. Great, she thought. A minion for Dingo. She swiped it roughly off the screen in a fit of impatience. The picture roll landed on the photo of the Singa-Sphynx Cat Rescue of the Deep South paperwork from Mavis' desk.

A glint caught Sabine's attention. She pinched her fingers outward to enlarge it. The ugly glass bowl on the desk reflected the names of the officers of the rescue. And that's when Sabine noticed. Dr. Mitchell Lana. His last name backward spelled anaL. The ass!

"Newt! Listen to this!" Sabine quickly outlined her theory of the "ass" from Kirby Morgan's list and Dr. Lana were the same person. She also explained Maxi Master's comment from church. "Kirby said that he had too many pests but he'd deal with an ass if Maxi could get rid of the bees. Newt, I can't explain it anymore, but my gut is saying Dr. Lana and Mavis are somehow wrapped up in this.

Newt nodded. "I can see that but the only thing we have is a bunch of loose threads. Let's call Mia and Lee and see if they want to come over to mull things over." He had learned to trust Sabine's investigative reporter instincts and Mia's knowledge of the community.

An hour later, with Dingo barking and Calvin lending her meow, Lee and Mia arrived bearing a bottle of wine and their small kitten peeking out from a pink purse adorned with purple rhinestones with a matching collar.

"Meet Shadow." A beaming Mia pulled out the purring kitten. "Shadow Jewel Kingsley to be exact. Lee is her legal father and I'm going to adopt her after the wedding. And don't you just love her collar? Pink and lavender will be her signature colors." She turned to Sabine. "What are her sister's colors? Have you decided on a proper diet? You want your children to have the best of everything."

"Well, nothing's been decided but I'm leaning toward a neon yellow since she's determined to be a dog." Sabine ignored Mia's scandalized look and dug in her cavernous purse to pull out her notebook and pen. "I've been holding this in for an hour. Let me tell you what happened at Dupont's." Sabine hurriedly related what transpired at the grocery store.

"WHAT? Lotta Hair is moving in my neighborhood? Oh, no she's not." Mia sprang from her seat and grabbed her car keys "We've got to do something! Like frame her or prove that she killed Kirby. She was probably one of the last people in the area to see him alive!"

Lee wrestled the keys away from Mia. "We'll deal with that situation in a bit."

When Mia sat mulishly down, Sabine prepared to write. "Let's talk people and timeline. First, we have a dead body. A married Kirby was last seen the night before at the Annual Chicken Daze Ball with Lottie McCall. The next day, he has an argument with Mr. Wallis at the Store concerning the land being fallow even though it really wasn't. Kirby called Maxi Master that afternoon hiring her to kill a bunch of angry bees for the next morning."

Newt took up the timeline drama. "Drayton met Maxi at the farm the next morning but Kirby was already gone. Drayton then called Ostie who actually did something by calling Mavis. Then during today's interview, Mavis said she and Kirby had gotten into a fight about the farm and how it offended her fruitarian sensibilities—something about how we won the genetic lottery. Then she claimed he took off to Africa and he hasn't been seen since. But Mavis stated he was pouting. I did find out that she is not legally involved with Kirby's business interests which add up to a significant amount of money. And money, according to Sabine's pictures, she is lacking."

Mia waded in. "Let's talk suspects. Mavis is the obvious choice, followed by the slimy vet. My dad told me to include him as one and I agreed only to calm him down enough to finish mowing the lawn. Then there's Drayton but I don't get that tingly feeling. And lastly, but certainly not least—Lottie McCall. Personally, I can see her doing him in because he probably dumped her after she ruined his radial arm saw with the hair of hers." Mia finished her diatribe against her mortal enemy as she stroked

Shadow's ears with one hand and Dingo with the other. “And another thing, why isn't she using my mother as her real estate broker? There is no one better in the region! It's listed with an agent in Hooks County.”

Lee leaned down to tend to a meowing Calvin. "Hon, let's focus on the case and then we'll talk about how to persuade Ms. Tilda to go with your mother. But I agree about Drayton. He's a good guy. He organizes the surrounding fire departments to enter the Pull a Delta Jet charity to raise money for cancer research and he does the lawn care for free for his church in Stonecypher in Hooks County. And, Mia,” Lee turned to his fiancée. “I think we can we can all agree to take Lottie of the list. There's no motive."

Mia's jaw set stubbornly. "Kirby probably told her he could not date anyone as disagreeable and follicly challenged as her. In a fit of rage, she smothered him with the God-awful frizz bomb she calls hair. Now she wants to ruin my parents' retirement."

Lee looked to Sabine for help but Sabine was assiduously avoiding eye contact. "Well, let's take Drayton off and Lottie is then way down on the list. Let's just focus on Mavis and Dr. Lana, okay Mia? I don't think Lottie has it in her genes to kill anyone except to maim your shoe collection."

Sabine's thoughts finally began coalescing. “Genes! The genetic lottery thing? Mavis said it during the interview. And Dr. Lana said that too during the $225 office visit. That's another thing. He has got to be up to his eyeballs. And oh, oh, oh!”

Sabine bounced up off the couch and started punching the air.

Lee's countenance showed extreme alarm as he too jumped up. "Oh, my God. Call 911 and tell Gina that Sabine's having some sort of seizure. I'll get my emergency bag from the truck. Ease her to the floor. Don't put anything in her mouth." He stared expectantly and then bewildered at Newt and Mia who both reclined further into their seats.

Mia pulled Lee back down. "No. She's not having a seizure. It's her thought process. As Momma described it, it's like Sabine's brain is constipated and all those little thoughts are finally breaking free to shoot out. Just let it go."

Lee returned to his chair and scanned the living room as if searching for prank cameras.

When Sabine finally regained the ability to speak coherently, she rushed out her realization. "Dr. Lana is bi-lingual. He speaks English and Spanish. I know because he called me a whore in Spanish. But he listed a university in Brazil as his veterinarian alma mater." Exasperated at the baffled expressions of her fellow Scooby Gang, she went on. "Brazil's national language is Portuguese, not Spanish. He should be able to carry on a conversation in Portuguese."

Realization dawned on Newt. "So the Ass is a liar? I would bet my last bottle of *Brännvin* that Dr. Lana is not a real doctor at all."

-27-

Squirrel meatloaf at our favorite diner.

"Oh, stink." Sabine started pacing and quickly pulled up the time in Brazil with her smart phone. "It's too late to check his record from his school down in South America."

Newt pulled on her hand. "Sit down and let's finish our timeline." When Sabine complied, he began again. "Snookie finds Kirby last week. We can't establish a cause of death, but Sabine finds an unused EpiPen belonging to Kirby fifty feet from the body. Kirby had a deathly allergy to bees, which necessitated the call to Maxi Masters."

"Lottie probably had a beehive in her hair..." Mia began snidely but closed her mouth after exasperated glances from all three.

"Sabine makes an appointment with Dr. Lana and finds out from the chatty receptionist that Mavis and Dr. Lana are in bed together, figuratively speaking. Mavis is supposedly the practice's main investor."

Lee scratched his head. "Didn't you just say, Newt, that Mavis has no money since Kirby locked her out of the business? But Mavis is the vet's money gal?"

Sabine interjected. "But two years ago, Madame Skank had access to money—Kirby's. She probably used the household money or her allowance from Kirby to do it. But since she didn't have access to ready cash since then, she was one mortgage payment away from pushing a Kroger buggy and searching for aluminum cans. That is until Kirby turned up dead and now she claims he had no will but I know for a fact she did. Does the will not leave her anything?"

"It boils down to why?" Mia tilted her head. "Why would she wait two years? Why lie about the will unless the money's not going to her? Mom said all the art and frou-frou knick-knacks were fake. The house was up for sale and as Sabine said, she was about to be out on her Chanel keister. She seemed to be okay with her hubby missing for all that time. Until Snookie dug up his arm, Kirby's whereabouts and health were unknown. Something or someone was forcing her to wait."

Newt stared off into the distance. "And all wasn't well at Skank Manor in Atlanta. Edweener found the cease and desist order as well as a petition for divorce. Maxi also said Kirby was living at the farm in that trailer that Edweener bought for a song. She said she did some renovations before Kirby left."

"Do you know if anyone has really searched that trailer?" Lee asked. "We still have a few hours of daylight left..."

Sabine's cell rang before plans were solidified. "Hello?"

"Sabine...is...you remember?" A twangy voice whispered.

"Who is this? You whispering too low."

"It's Dee from Dr. Lana's office."

"Yep. Of course. Why are you whispering?"

"Because I'm hiding under my desk at the office."

"Why are..."

Dee took a short breath. "I came back in when I saw I left my wallet here. One of the Girl Scouts visited my townhouse and I had to buy those Thin Mints. You know those cookies? To die for! Chop them up on vanilla ice cream..."

Sabine interrupted. "I know what Thin Mints are but that doesn't explain why you're hiding and whispering."

"I overheard Mavis and the Ass arguing. I couldn't make out all what they were saying but he was yelling about a will and money and Kirby's name was brought up a few times. I ducked under the desk when she stormed out. He grabbed her arm and pulled her back. Now he's still yelling but Mavis is silent. Mavis is NEVER silent. Not gonna lie to you Sabine. I'm a little scared of him right now. He yelled at me the afternoon after your appointment. He demanded to know why someone from Jaemore County would come see him. I told him I didn't know but he snatched your file from my desk and marched out."

"Can you crawl out and get to the police?" Sabine's stomach fluttered in anxiety. Dee's fright was palatable through the phone.

"And tell them what? He may be assaulting Mavis? And if you think Mavis is going to back me up, you're wrong. She has that stupid reputation to protect. He knows where I live. I mean, my dad and sisters are safe. They're back in India celebrating Dussehra. But I couldn't take off this year so I'm all alone at my townhouse. He's even got your address."

"Then come out to my house and we'll get you a safe place for the night. My best friend's house has plenty of room and I'm sure you can stay there. Can you do that? It's a hike but I think that's your best bet. Right now, we have the best protection. A cop boyfriend, an evil Aussie, an attitude, and a gun."

"Yeah. I can do that. Text me your address. I'm already crawling out the door and can't look it up on the computer. I'll call in sick tomorrow with something contagious."

"Of course, and don't even stop for clothes. We'll deal when you get here." Sabine waited until Dee was driving away, pressed end and relayed the conversation to Newt, Mia and Lee.

Newt immediately sprang into action and called a friend in law enforcement that policed the area around Dr. Lana's office.

"While we're waiting, let's make a quick dinner." Sabine attempted to maintain normalcy.

"Yeah, and at the same time, we'll decide Calvin's go-to color and make sure we frame Lottie for something." Mia offered.

"Let's make supper and then finish fleshing out the case instead." Lee said as he rubbed his hands together. "We have a maybe fake but violent vet, a neurotic society maven, squirrel meatloaf at our favorite diner, a dead hubby skeleton, a missing will, overdue bills and now a fleeing vet tech. If this doesn't scream Jaemore County, nothing else will."

-28-

Or even having gas after eating verything in sight.

Despite offering to make a casserole of fermented herring, Newt hurriedly grilled hamburgers while Sabine and Mia peeled potatoes for French fries. Poor klutzy Lee was relegated to keeping the animals, Dingo in particular, occupied during food prep.

"How about blue and bronze for Calvin's colors?" Mia suggested.

"Mia, this kitten doesn't need signature colors. She's basically a dog wrapped in a cute little feline body."

Mia shook her head. "It's short sided parental thinking like yours that keeps me busy investigating neglect."

"It's crazy ass thinking like yours that keeps me pulling out my hair. Next you'll want to know if we started a college fund."

Mia scrunched her face and threw a potato peeling at Sabine. "Fuddy-duddy."

"Such language. Helicopter parent." Sabine launched more potato peels at Mia.

"Before you two start the Great Potato Peel War, Duncan, my cop friend from Buckhead, just called. Both Mavis and Lana were at the office. Neither had any marks or blood on them. They both denied any argument." Newt stuck his head in the kitchen. "Duncan said some neighbors called to complain so Dee is off the hook for now."

The facts and theories were rehashed over dinner and despite overwhelming evidence, Mia still was firmly entrenched in the blame Lotta Hair arena. It was the consensus that Dr. Lana was the most promising suspect but Mavis was running a close second as a complicit person of interest.

Newt ran his fingers through this thinning blonde hair. "What we need is to get our hands on a copy of Kirby's will. And who is the executor of this? Surely, it's not Mavis. Especially if Kirby was filing for divorce through Hamilton Bilbo. And who are the witnesses? What attorney prepared it? This has made the national news. We got phone calls from New York newspapers, websites and network news. Bilbo told me he does not touch probate matters, especially wills, so he doesn't have the will."

Sabine slapped her head. "If only, I took a better picture of the will at Castle Skank. I cut off the signatures to get the first half of the back page."

Lee kindly peeled Sabine's hand off her forehead. "Sabine, it's lucky you snapped a picture of the will at all. And we are all thinking that an attorney did the will. Kirby may have written the will himself. Self-written will examples are all over the internet."

Dingo choose that moment to begin a barking campaign and waddled to the front door. Her feline cohort, Calvin, also meowed fiercely.

The doorbell rang and the barking turned to brisk butt wiggling. Newt casually placed his hand on his service pistol and opened the door to a heavily breathing Dee, clutching a box of Thin Mints and a large purse.

"I bring gifts!" She held the cookies and smiled. Newt took the box and Dee squatted in front of Dingo for a quick round of belly rubs. "Oh, who are you?" She scooped up Calvin who batted fiercely at her and hugged the kitten. "You look just like the kitty cat I grew up with!"

"Thank you for putting me up." Dee began after all the introductions were made. "I've been thinking of quitting for two years and this was the final straw. I'm calling in tomorrow and giving my notice. I'm not even going to work two weeks. That fight scared the bejesus out of me."

"You're welcome to stay here as long as you need." Mia assured her. "Consider Jaemore County your Witness Protection Location".

Dee grinned. "It already feels like home."

The doorbell dinged again. This time, Shadow jumped out of Mia's lap and joined her sister and Dingo at announcing a new visitor.

Mia scooped up her kitten. "Tell your dog to quit it. I don't want her to pick Dingo's bad habits like making loud noises or drinking vodka. Or even having gas after eating everything in sight."

Newt opened the front door again with his hand on his holster, only to be towered over by a grim Drayton.

"I've been thinking." Drayton stomped in without looking at anyone. "Kirby was my boss and even though he was stubborn, he was a friend. I've been racking my brain over the last week I saw Kirby..." Drayton halted near Lee and stared at Dee who, in turn, shifted her eyes to Sabine, clearly embarrassed by Drayton's gaze.

"I'm Dhwani, but you can call me Dee." Dee shifted a kitten off her lap and extended her hand.

At Lee's prodding, Drayton grasped Dee's. His giant hand enveloped her tiny one. "It's nice to meet you, Dee. I'm Drayton. Drayton Wilcox. I have to say that you have the most beautiful brown eyes." She quickly averted his scrutiny as if flustered.

"Thank you." A blushing Dee cut her eyes back to Sabine who was enjoying both of their discomfort. "Why don't you have a seat beside me and tell us what got you so riled up?"

Drayton dropped his smile as he remembered why he stormed in. "I was driving on Highway 316 this afternoon after taking a proctored midterm at UGA. I don't know why but I yelled 'Yellow Car' when a yellow Nissan pulled out in front of me near the Gwinnett County line. I started thinking about the times Kirby and I would be driving to pick up something for the farm and we played 'Yellow Car.'"

"'Yellow Car?' I'm not following you." Dee tilted her head.

Drayton shook his head. "It was a stupid game we played to pass the time on the road. Not many cars are yellow and we'd see who could find the most yellow cars during the trip. The loser would buy lunch."

"Okay, still not seeing why this required a trip out here." Sabine motioned impatiently.

"The last time we played 'Yellow Car' was the day before he disappeared. We were driving back from Greenleaf and we passed a yellow car pulling out from the farm. At the time, we just thought the driver was turning around, but it stands out because it was one of those "environmentally friendly" cars that you don't see in rural Georgia. It was..."

"A yellow Prius with a blue racing stripe?" Dee finished. "That's Dr. Lana's car. Fool idiot putting a racing stripe on a wind-up clown car."

Drayton nodded. Everyone was silent, digesting the information.

"That means Dr. Lana's car was probably in the vicinity of the farm." Drayton finished.

Newt's jaw clenched. "I'm going to find out everything about this guy if I have to wake up the entire nation of Brazil."

Sabine handed Calvin to him. "Let's start fresh tomorrow morning. Dee's had a long drive and everyone is tired. And Calvin needs to bond with you more. Everyone go home and we'll regroup tomorrow morning at 9 at Mrs. Wallis' real estate office. She's got a conference room, wireless, and a kick butt espresso maker."

Mia couldn't resist a parting shot. "Who died and made you the calm one?"

*29-

Inducting herself in the birthplace of the Whack-A-Doodle Hall of Fame.

Sabine was late. Newt had left bright and early to get a start on calling the vet school in Brazil. Calvin purred contentedly on Newt's pillow while Sabine raced around and realized she did not rinse the shampoo out of her. Dingo took the opportunity to steal her bra which followed a chase through the house and ultimately out the doggie door. Sabine surrendered and put on her itchy camisole bra and one of Newt's sweatshirts to counteract the cooler fall air and left Dingo to chew the cups out of Sabine's favorite Over the Shoulder Boulder Holder bra.

Sabine stopped short at the site of her canine guttersnipe and chewed lingerie near her car. Dingo had raced out the back doggie door, sailed over the back fence and planted herself near the Challenger when Sabine turned after locking her front door.

"You're not going." Sabine stood her ground. "You don't like my driving. You always complain about it. Get back to the backyard."

Dingo yawned as the bra caught on a molar and pointedly turned her head to stare out the Challenger.

"Now I know why Labradors, not Australian Shepherds are the most popular breed in the country. Labradors love and obey their owners, unlike Aussies." Sabine surrendered and opened the door for Dingo to jump into the car. "Please do not change the radio or drool too much. I had to spray down the windows after that trip to Atlanta."

Once in Greenleaf and after maneuvering into a tight spot, Sabine switched off the car and opened the driver's door. Dingo clamored over her owner to be the first one in the real estate office.

Arial Bixby opened the door for a dignified Dingo to stroll into the building. Sabine was struck at how Arial blossomed under Mrs. Wallis' tutelage. Arial had gained much needed weight and the dark circles under her eyes had all but vanished. Pictures of her children, Kayla and Dion, graced her tidy desk along with a small picture of her and Mick Jaemore smiling and mugging for the camera with Six Flags over Georgia amusement park in the background.

"Good morning, Sabine." Arial smiled. "Mrs. Wallis and everyone is already in the conference room."

Sabine started. When they first met, Arial was abrupt and hostile. Granted, she had just been drugged and informed that her children had been placed in foster care, but Arial seemed to have developed an intense dislike for Sabine in particular. In ensuing months, a détente had developed. Dion had stopped sticking his tongue out at her and Sabine refrained from making faces.

"Thanks, Arial." Sabine trailed behind her dog, who was no doubt in search of Krispy Kreme donuts and other pastries.

The conference room was full. Drayton, Lee, and Newt were murmuring together while Mia had commandeered the laptop and was on eBay placing a bid for a vintage pair of sunglasses. Mrs. Wallis and Dee were deep in conversation over a diagram of a house. Dingo snuck under the table and poked her head through on Newt's lap for a quick scratch. Sabine snagged an empty chair near Newt.

"That's a beautiful house." Dee exclaimed loudly. "And the price is perfect! I'll take it!"

Heads swiveled toward Dee and Mrs. Wallis, who were both beaming brightly.

"Mrs. Wallis and I were talking late into the night. Y'all know I'm not going back to the vet clinic. Thanks to her, I'm going to buy Jaemore Manor and turn it into a bed and breakfast inn! I emailed my notice to Dr. Lana and the other vets this morning telling them I will mail my keys to them. I even told them not to worry about paying vacation out or anything. One of the vet techs said she'd pack my stuff and leave it at my house."

Sabine was sure she was not the only one stunned at the quick change of events. She didn't want to burst Dee's bubble and tell her she was voluntarily inducting herself in the birthplace of the Whack-A-Doodle Hall of Fame.

As everyone congratulated Dee, Newt whispered in his girlfriend's ear. "Sabine, you might want to get rid of that dirty bra hooked to your shoe."

Sabine surreptitiously bent and yanked the bra from her sneakers. She bundled it up to toss when she realized everyone was already staring at her.

"Come on. Go ahead and toss that bra." Mia rolled her eyes. "You don't have it in you to be sneaky."

Dee's contagious happiness infected everyone. "It's gonna be an adventure and I'll need lots of help, particularly getting the outside into shape. Denise says the inside is pretty much taken care of but the lawn has been neglected over the past few years." Dee went on. "I'm going to combine my mom's Indian cooking with good old-fashioned Southern lard and love."

"Don't forget the white dirt." Mrs. Wallis interjected as she gracefully perched on the chair at the head of the table like she was the Chairman of the Joint Chiefs of Staff in the White House underground war room. "Let's get this started. The sooner Dr. Lana is off the streets, the better."

"I placed a call to the university that Lana claims he graduated from and I'm waiting to hear from them. When I get back to the office, I'll dig around Mavis Augustine's background a little deeper." Newt offered.

"Mia and I can poke around Kirby's repo'd trailer." Sabine offered.

Mia shook her head. "I can't. I'm way behind at work and even now Lennie, my horrid supervisor, thinks I'm on a case."

"I'll go." Dee raised her hand. "The bank where all my investments are in India won't open for a few hours."

Lee piped up as he read his email on his smartphone. "I'm a no go also. I've been called to Rosa's Thrift Store. Apparently, Elvis Lyons thought it would be funny to hide a stink bomb in the faux fur coat section. Rosa caught him with ammonia and sulfur. Since they're semi-toxic, she's insisting that the Fire Chief dispose of the remains while MeeMaw takes care of Elvis."

All the adults except for Dee and Drayton frowned and shifted uncomfortably. When you put a seventy-year-old grandmother in charge of discipline, there was bound to be sore bottoms and possibly hard labor. When one of her older grandchildren, Tucker Johnson, was arrested for underage drinking and possession of meth at a state park, Tucker pleaded with the Park Rangers and Drug Enforcement Agency to be sentenced to prison. Instead, they released him to MeeMaw who promptly went angry grandma supernova on him. It was rumored that Tucker used an inflatable ring pillow for three weeks after that.

Drayton broke the uncomfortable silence. "I'll go with you two. You might need some heavy lifting." The group knew this was a thinly veiled ploy to stay with Dee. Drayton's eyes never left Dee's face. It was clear that Drayton was already falling hard for the new Jaemore County resident. Dee, for her part, was clueless to the handsome giant.

"Just don't disturb anything too much." Newt warned. "I want anything preserved for evidence, if I need it." Newt swung to face Sabine and Dingo. "And you, young lady, try to stay in one piece and out of trouble. No wandering around or running amok. I don't want to get another phone call."

Sabine frowned. "I have Dingo's leash. She won't get loose again."

"I'm not concerned about the Aussie. I was referring to you."

-30-

Make my VW Beetle a four-wheel drive car with custom designed mud flaps.

"You are such a sweet girl." Dee crooned in the back seat of the Challenger as she rubbed Dingo's backside.

If Dee was in her element scratching a dog, Drayton was a Nervous Nellie. He was stiffly sitting in the front seat, staring ahead silently, trying his best not to glance back at Dee.

Sabine made a jab at small talk. "Drayton, you said you're getting your master's degree. What's it in? How far along are you?"

"Uhm..." Drayton licked his lips. "I'm getting it in Cyber Security. I'm due to graduate this December. I hope to get on with the GBI in their Computer Crimes division or maybe one of those cops who chase down internet pedophiles or computer forensics. You know, something that doesn't have a lot of blood in it."

"Why?" Dee cocked her head. "Aren't you a fire fighter?"

Drayton sheepishly turned to the back seat. "Well, I do a lot of fire education at the schools and I can help people especially children but the sight of blood and guts makes me faint."

"Oh, my oldest sister, Krisha, is like that too." Dee tilted her head and fell silent for several seconds. "It's too bad. Krisha was always good in science. She'd make a great doctor or...vet." Dee ceased her dialogue abruptly and brought her right fist to her mouth.

Sabine caught the imperceptible break. "What's going on in that head?"

Dee shifted and leaned forward. "I never put the pieces together. The Tuxedo clinic has four veterinarians so it's a busy place. I've been the office manager for three years so I'm not in the day-to-day practice like when I was a vet tech. Lana has not, in the two years he's been there, taken a case where the animal needs to be operated on or actually hurt. He does the wellness checkups, but the vet technician gives the shots. Dr. Lana comes in basically to push his over the top dog or cat food. No one knows anything about him. He's intensely personal and everyone hates talking to him."

Drayton cocked his head. "He doesn't actually treat animals?"

Sabine clenched her jaw. "He charges $225 to hawk his dog food?"

"Yes, and it sells like wildfire." Dee confirmed. "With Mavis behind him and twisting other badly dyed arms, he's making a tidy profit from it. Some owners buy hundreds of dollars without blinking an eye. I could make my VW Beetle a four-wheel drive car with custom designed mud flaps." Dee stopped talking and pondered the actual benefits of turning her Beetle into a monster vehicle with giant tires.

"What's so special about it?" Drayton asked.

Dee shook her head. "Nothing. I fed some to my dad's golden retriever, Hiran, when Dr. Lana started selling it about a year ago. Looks and smells just like regular old dog chow to me. After a month on it, I didn't notice any change in digestion nor did Hiran's coat get any shiner. It's a scam, but I figure I can run interference and maybe save some pets by routing them to the other doctors in the practice as much as I can."

Sabine clicked on her blinker to turn into the driveway where Edweener's trailers were. She had a quick flashback of fending off Lindy Mills and her designer roach killer shoes with ragweed but she shoved that back down in her memories. Lindy Mills was presently incarcerated in a South Georgia women's prison for twenty-five years to serve. Not surprisingly, she was also convicted of attempted murder and cruelty to children. Sabine purposefully returned her thoughts to the present.

"Here we are." Sabine put the car in park and thanked God for the clear weather. Red clay, water and mud did not mix well the first time she drove down here.

Dingo immediately squatted and left her calling card all the while sniffing the air for clues. Dee crinkled her nose at the unkempt homes but recovered quickly. Drayton was used to seeing poverty and filth and was immune to it. He needed no instruction and strode to the pink trailer.

Drayton held out his hand to help Dee onto the crumbling steps. "Dee, be careful. This mobile home has not been taken care of. There are holes in the floor and God knows what animals are living in there."

Dingo needed no invitation and sprinted up the stairs. Sabine rounded up the rear and cautiously entered the trailer. To her left, she saw the untouched kitchen where Dee was using an old utensil to poke around the area. She detected Drayton's mutterings in the back bedroom where Kirby's office was. Following Dee's lead, Sabine grabbed a wayward stick and pried open cabinets under the bar. Other than discovering an abandoned nest of field mice among empty liquor bottles, Sabine came up empty.

Sabine sat back on her knees and absently scratched a nosy Dingo. "What am I missing?"

With that, Dingo took off, rounding the corner back to Drayton's location, barking fiercely.

Sabine grimaced at the popping of her knee joints and hurried to find her errant dog. Dingo was hanging out of the doorway to the bathroom snarling and growling. Sabine uprooted Dingo back and peered around the corner. She barely spied the new jacuzzi tub Maxi had installed. The next site was of a frightened skunk. Sabine pivoted in an attempt to avert full body coverage but still was awarded with an oily spray on her shirt.

"What the..." Drayton careened around the corner and immediately pinched his nose shut while Dee closed in from the opposite side.

"Is everything...Oh my goodness, who stopped up...Ack!" Dee whipped toward the hallway wall as the scared skunk scampered past to safety. Dingo slunk back to Dee and wrapped around her legs.

Drayton, still holding his nose, said. "Uh, Sabine, you stay in the bathroom while Dee holds on to Dingo. I'm going to call Lee to have him come up with his truck. I pretty sure you don't want to drive home. You know in an enclosed space with fabric or anywhere there are living beings who need oxygen. Just my two scents, though." Drayton finished his pun in a whoosh to breathe through his mouth.

Sabine's shoulders drooped. "This is going to haunt me forever, isn't it?"

"In the annals of history." Dee could not contain a giggle as she backed away with the Aussie.

"Cheer up, Sabine. Your in-stinks were on the money." Drayton's belly laugh and subsequent wall pounding shook the dilapidated trailer.

A split second later, a bang sounded behind Sabine. When she whipped around, the service cover to the bathtub fell open, spilling several sealed plastic bags. Ignoring the uncontrollable laughter behind her, Sabine pulled out her phone. Her pulse ignited when she read the last page of Kirby Morgan's Last Will and Testament dated two weeks before Kirby's disappearance. She gingerly moved the will slightly with her foot to discover a well-used journal.

"Yep, Drayton, you better call Newt too. We found Kirby's will!"

***

The first order of business was to load a highly smelly Sabine into the back of Lee's truck without contaminating anyone else who arrived. This included not only Newt and other first responders but Regina Bethesda, the local newspaper's owner and publisher as well as several of The Store's senior elderly patrons. Sabine was dismayed to see Lottie McCall snapping pictures for posterity. The 911 scanner was in fine force today. One of Lee's firefighters affixed an oxygen tank and hazmat suit on Newt who was determined to recover Kirby Morgan's paperwork from the odorous bathroom. Sabine had waved Newt away and only spoke to him by yelling twenty feet upwind.

If it were any other time, Sabine would enjoy the cool Georgia fall air on her face. Instead, there was the smell of burned rubber mixed with sulphur and a dash of old cabbage to deal with, as well as Drayton's running commentary with Lee through the open back window, interspersed with stink puns. Although Sabine was the only one to receive a full blast of skunk oil, Dee and Drayton were peripheral victims and had been barely dusted with the stink. The only member of the group to escape totally was Dingo, who again was in the Challenger's front seat being chauffeured by one of Jaemore County's finest to the house like Queen Elizabeth returning to Buckingham Palace after a stag hunting party.

Fortunately, as a first responder, Lee knew what to do or, in this case, who to call. One conversation with Mrs. Wallis gave Lee a recipe from Granny Lureen guaranteed to de-skunk Sabine. Sadly, Newt's sweatshirt was a casualty from the skunk attack. Sabine shivered slightly after only being covered with her camisole while they drove to the Wallis' house. Mrs. Wallis would be the only one in the area who had hydrogen peroxide, baking soda and dishwashing detergent in reserve to clean three adults.

"Hey, Sabine!" Dee shouted excitedly. "Sally Jackson, that reporter from Channel 7, is live streaming a report from the Animal Farm, right now. She's in rare form. She talked to Mavis, who insulted Kirby, Jaemore County, and Newt. He's not talking to her and now she's blasting the sheriff's office about a conspiracy and a federal lawsuit of some sort."

Sabine's blood pressure shot up, and then she grinned evilly. They would be passing the farm on their right a few minutes before the Skunk-Mobile arrived at the Wallis'. "Drayton, tell Lee to slow down. I want to get a good look at the farm."

Drayton relayed the message, and in a few seconds, the ostentatious Channel 7 News Van came into view. It partially blocked the road and driveway, squatting like a leviathan. Lee skillfully dodged the wires and narrowly missed the fender by driving off the road.

"Yo, Sally!" Sabine swung Newt's smelly sweatshirt in the air as if she was the main attraction at a low-end strip club near Hartsfield-Jackson Airport in south Fulton and Clayton counties. Sabine let go of the shirt when Sally glanced around the van with her news camera operator following her line of vision with his equipment. Just as Sabine's idol, Dallas Cowboy Roger Staubach found Drew Pearson in the 1975 playoff game against the Vikings, her aim was true and the shirt landed on Sally's head.

"Insult Newt again and you'll get the whole skunk." Sabine hollered as Lee righted the truck and drove away. "Kirby Morgan deserves more to be the subject of your tabloid journalism."

"Got it all on video." Dee whooped like a proper redneck from Greenleaf. "I'm uploading it to YouTube right now. I hope it goes viral. That's what she gets for dissing my new hometown."

Sabine's cell phone rang and she was heartened to see Newt's number flash. "Hey, I was just defending your honor." She informed him of her snarky yet effective revenge on Jaemore's Most Hated Fake News Reporter.

"Well, I looked at Kirby's Will. All of Kirby's assets are to go a new non-profit called the Morgan Historical Restoration Foundation. He wants this new entity to award grants to small historical societies or museums that get overlooked usually or overshadowed by the more well-known societies and I quote 'like the Higgens Museum of Modern Art.' One of Kirby's witnesses was a doctor who died four months after he signed it and the other was just a bank notary from Fulton County who passed away last month. No one could say anything about a dated will when they all were dead. Get this—Drayton is the executor, and, in the will, Kirby asked that Drayton be hired as the first director of the foundation." Newt finished excitedly.

"Ooohh...burn on Mavis. She's a docent for the Higgens Museum. Such a slap in the orange tanned face." Sabine giggled. "What can I do to be in the room when you tell Mavis? I'll even eat pickled herring."

"First, get de-stinked. I'm going to read Kirby's journal and then we'll celebrate in style."

"Does that mean a cherry Icee?" Sabine bounced up and down. She finished the conversation and caught Dee staring at her.

"Do you really get excited about getting an Icee?"

"Yeah, you'll find out that excitement is slim pickings here."

"Oh, honey. That's fine. After the past few days, I need some calm time." Dee grinned.

-31-

Do they belong to PISSY?

Mrs. Wallis motioned for the trio to get out of the truck bed. "Y'all boys just stay where you are. Ladies, if you can make your way without touching anything, and I mean, *anything* to the back yard, I put a bucket of Granny Lureen's Anti-Skunk Neutralizer. Strip to your undies and paste it on yourself. Leave it on for fifteen minutes and holler." She turned to go back into the house. "Lee, park that truck on the street. With any luck, the wind will whip the smell out of your truck bed and into Mrs. Hughes' yard."

When Sabine and Dee arrived on the patio, Dee sniffed at the pail. "What's in here?"

Sabine shrugged. "You know, I stopped asking questions like that a long time ago. I've come to the realization it's just best not to ask because you really won't like the answer. But one thing is for sure: either Granny Lureen was a mad scientist or a certifiable genius level doctor. Every recipe or saying from her rings true or tastes out of this world."

After the requisite wait time and spray down, Mrs. Wallis pronounced them deodorized enough to come into the house and handed them her son Caleb's hand me down sweats.

To Sabine's surprise, Newt was in the midst of a discussion with Mr. Wallis, the newest graduate of the Constantinople Academy of Criminal Justice in Kingston, Jamaica, about the dilemma of the shrinking trunk space in American model sedans and how that affects a serial killer's modus operandi. Newt finally held his hand up to halt Mr. Wallis' rather lengthy conclusion of searching all foreign car trunks during traffic stops for dead bodies.

"You don't smell!" Newt grinned as he placed a quick peck on his girlfriend's forehead.

"You're surprised? Do I always stink or something?" Sabine wrinkled her nose.

"You know that's not what I mean. I have to give a statement to Regina from the Jaemore Journal as a follow-up. You're hot news, Sabine."

"Because I got sprayed?"

"No. You found Kirby's Will and Testament and his personal journal. Have a seat and I'll give some highlights. We're just waiting for Mia to show up."

"Ask and you shall receive." Mia sauntered in and scooted beside Lee. "I finished all the investigations today and I found out Arial's child protective services and foster care case has been closed. I was so excited that I hand delivered the closure letter to her." Last spring, when Sabine found Arial unconscious, Mia had no choice but to place Arial's two children in foster care but with some luck and hard work by everyone, the children were returned. Arial no longer was in need of support services and effectively "graduated" from DFCS.

When everyone settled, Sabine noticed Drayton had made his way near Dee and was perched on the hearth. It was quite noticeable that Drayton was over the moon for Dee.

Newt outlined the will and waited several minutes for a shell-shocked Drayton to recover from Kirby's last act.

"He always said he'd help me whenever he could." Drayton was close to tears. "I just didn't think it would be like this."

"That's not all. He left Lottie his mother's engagement ring and something called a diamond lavalliere. I have no clue what that is. I'm sure Mavis will never surrender that ring and diamond thing." Newt did indeed look perplexed. English still gave him fits. He missed the knowing look between Mia and Sabine. "Most of the journal contained notes and figures for the restoration of the cabin. He was inordinately proud that the chimney and hearth had been repaired per instructions from the Georgia Trust for Historic Preservation."

Newt shifted his seat. "Has anyone heard of PFFT?" He studied everyone expectantly. "No? Neither had I until I researched it. PFFT stands for Planetary Friends For Tomorrow. It's a shady animal rights group whose mission statement is 'We believe that all life is valuable. Just because humans won the genetic lottery by developing thumbs doesn't mean we can impose our value and thought system on other sentient beings.' Sound familiar?"

"OOOhhhh. Dr. Lana is always spouting off that!!" Dee jumped up at the same time Sabine did.

"Mavis Augustine said that during the interview!" Sabine said. "Don't you remember, Newt? Don't you? Do they belong to PISSY?" She grabbed Newt's arm tightly.

"Calm down. It's PFFT, not pissy." Newt peeled her off. "I do remember. I was there!"

Drayton interjected. "Shady? Are they eco-terrorists? It seems to me that the Ass has the personality to be sneaky."

Newt shook his head. "Not shady like that. Shady like crook shady. PFFT's 501 (c) status has been revoked by the IRS twice and it is not allowed to fund raise in four states due to some fraudulent dealing. My guess is that PFFT is a front to scam people, especially wealthy people, out of some money. I've not had a lot of time, what with the skunk incident, dealing with Sally Jackson who, by the way, smells to high heaven, and talking to the university in Brazil."

"I'm on PFFT." Mia whipped out her phone, her experience in uncovering online sales legendary and glared at Sabine. "Give me ten minutes, tops."

"And go." Sabine started the stopwatch on her phone. From the bewildering looks she received, she explained. "It's a thing with us. We watch Antiques Roadshow and whoever gets closest to the Keno

Brothers' estimate without going over wins a Tootsie Roll. Mia and I are Google experts."

"What did the Brazil people say?" Lee asked.

"Mitchell Lana is not a graduate of their program. They have no record of him at all." Newt pronounced. "Sabine was right to be suspicious of him."

"Dee also remembered that Lana never did any actual vet stuff." Sabine supplied.

Dee took it from there. "He never gave the animals shots or performed thorough wellness checkups."

Sabine, cheap as she was, couldn't let go of the memory of the pricey dog food. "Drayton, do you know anyone at UGA or who is involved in animal feed who will test the dog food from Lana's line? I'd be willing to bet that's a scam too."

"GOT IT! And under seven minutes!" Mia whooped loudly.

"Yes, yes. A new record for my princess." Mrs. Wallis said drily. "What do you have?"

Mia could barely contain herself. "PFFT has a failing grade from that website which governs transparency and information for non-profits as well as a horrible rating from the Better Business Bureau. Newt's hypothesis was right. There are four states—California, Nevada, Texas and West Virginia—that have either investigated or are still investigating PFFT as a phony scam charity. Mitchell Lana is listed as the principal officer with a governing board in Brazil. One name is the president of Universidade Integradas Plinio Leite, which I bet the Brazil dude doesn't even know about."

"What else does Kirby write about PISSY?" Sabine nudged Newt.

"PFFT, not PISSY." Newt corrected her again. "Kirby believed PFFT was the driving force behind the defamation lawsuit–you know, the one that Edweener brought over. He couldn't prove it but he thought Lana put Mavis up to it. Kirby knew that Mavis was being influenced by Lana to funnel Kirby's money to PFFT and in turn, into Lana's pockets. One of his last entries said he had proof that PFFT was a shady organization. Kirby even suspected PFFT was responsible for the animal breakout, as everyone knows, caused the farm to completely go under. He couldn't prove that though."

"What proof on PFFT did he have?" Sabine inquired.

"Sabine, if I knew that, I'd get arrest warrants." Newt's phone dinged and he excused himself to answer it.

Mr. Wallis boomed in. "That's right. You could get him on theft, which is 2-4 years." After that, he promptly shut his eyes to take a nap.

"What's next?" Drayton kept shaking his head. "We need to find hard confirmation. I say we get Mitchell Lana in and beat the crap out of him."

"If I could, I would, but he's gone." Newt returned. "He's disappeared along with Mavis. Mavis' house has been burglarized and several items were taken according to my counterparts in Buckhead. The maid called it in and left. Apparently, she's on probation for shoplifting an entire Thanksgiving dinner for eight a year ago from Whole Foods and didn't want to mess with "the man" as the landscaper said. The Prius was left at the house but Mavis' BMW 535 is missing."

"Please tell me someone knocked over Mavis' Man in Rapture statue and damaged it beyond repair!" Mrs. Wallis exclaimed.

"Did the financially strapped Mavis put her up to it?" Sabine asked.

Drayton submitted his theory. "Maybe the maid had a bunch of kids and had no money because Mavis hadn't paid her."

Mia was not to be left out. "I bet Lottie McCall something to do with that."

Newt rubbed his head and wished for a minor aneurysm.

-32-

Dingo, you are Albert Einstein wrapped in a matted fur coat.

"I am sleeping on the couch and that's final!" Lee stubbornly ordered, crossing his arms. "That Lana guy is probably very dangerous."

"No one knows Dee is here. You know, in my house." Mia explained. "Anyway, Daddy has enough guns to arm Seal Team Six. We're fine. Go home and sleep in a real bed."

Sabine intervened. "Dee can sleep at our house. Newt is there. We have a great guard dog and the attack kitten. Anyway, Mr. Wallis won't let Lee spend the night here. Remember Southern Daddy?"

In the end, Dee accompanied Newt and Sabine back to their house where a miffed Aussie totally ignored the adults who left her alone and concentrated all her attention on the new kitten.

"She'll come around in the middle of the night. But I'm so keyed up. I'm going to read a bit to calm down." Sabine shooed both Dee and Newt to bed. She perused her massive library of books that included a diverse array from recent bestsellers to her complete set of old Nancy Drew mysteries. It was Nancy Drew who became Sabine's idol, so it was only natural that she pulled "The Ghost of Blackwood Hall" from its spot.

Curled up on the couch with a quilt, her Aussie, and new kitten, Sabine fell asleep before she made to the end where Nancy received accolades for her keen insight and exceptional detective skills.

"Hey sleepyhead." Newt nudged Sabine gently. "I'm leaving for work."

Sabine blinked her eyes open. Dingo had wrapped herself around Sabine's legs and Calvin had made a bed on her neck.

"Sleepyhead? I feel like Dr. Doolittle." Sabine squinted at the cable box time. It was still dark outside but the sun was quickly dawning with the promise of a perfect Georgia fall day.

"I'm going to have the road deputies patrol out here so don't be alarmed. I had to pull a couple from night shift. They'll be in their personal cars because we just don't have the extra autos. I'm not trying to catch you doing something illegal or outrageous although I wouldn't be surprised if you end up in handcuffs one of these days. It's to make sure Lana doesn't come around." Newt bent to kiss her cheek, mindful of morning breath mixed with dog saliva. "If you go somewhere, take your gun or Dingo."

Sabine waved Newt off and felt the animals leap off the couch to go outside for their morning constitutionals via the doggy door. She must have dozed off when she heard Dee in the kitchen making magical breakfast items. The smell of vanilla and apples beckoned Sabine and she found herself in line for begging.

"I don't have the poor doggy eyes or kitten ears but could I get some of whatever deliciousness you have coming out of the oven?" Sabine pleaded as she folded the quilt and set her Nancy Drew book on an empty chair in the kitchen.

"Of course." Dee scooped up a helping of food. "It's called Apple Halwa. It's made from apples but all you had was canned apple pie filling so I improvised. I found a few pecans out under your pecan tree and shelled them. I used them instead of almonds. I hope it's okay. I was thinking about using this recipe for the bed and breakfast inn."

Sabine inhaled it faster than Dingo finding a prime rib. "Oh. My. God. Girl you are a flipping genius in the kitchen. If you ever should need a guinea pig, I will be your go-to rodent. No payment needed."

Dee placed another helping in front of Sabine and sat down with her own breakfast. "What's on the agenda?" Dee casually picked up the Nancy Drew book. "I loved Nancy. My favorite was the Old Clock but I loved this one too. I used to race ahead to the end to see which mystery Nancy would have next."

Dee idly flipped to the last page. "The Clue in the Leaning Chimney. I don't remember this one."

With great difficulty, Sabine ceased eating. "What did you say?"

"Just that I loved Nancy Drew. Why?"

"No. No. Something just triggered a memory." Sabine tapped her fingers impatiently. Calvin took the tapping as an invitation to claw Sabine's thumb. "Stop it, Calvin. I have to think."

Dingo nosed the book from Dee's hand and woofed gently.

"That's it! Dingo, you are Albert Einstein wrapped in a matted fur coat. Chimney!" Sabine whooped loudly, stood up and punched the air.

"Yes, that's what I said." Dee cautiously said. "Are you having an allergic reaction to the pecans? Or the apples? Do you take medication in the morning? Are you on to something?"

"No. No. No. Yes." Sabine flopped back down. "Everyone has been saying how Kirby really took to the restoration process. When he found out that the old homestead was on the property, he started learning the skills needed to restore everything including the chimney. Both Drayton and Lottie McCall pointed out that he was inordinately proud of the chimney and how he used the same materials and process to rebuild it like it was in the 19th century."

"Yes, I remember Drayton saying something like that." Dee leaned in further as if sensing a momentous announcement.

"Don't you see? Kirby recreated the chimney just like it was when it was built. A chimney like that always had a hidey hole. It was usually for a safe place to keep valuables before safes and security systems became available. What if Kirby built a hidden niche and placed pictures or a paper trail that implicated PFFT in shady deals."

"That's a stretch, Sabine. But we got nothing else. Let's go."

Sabine showered and dressed in record time. She quickly texted Newt about her theory as she and Dee slid into the Challenger. Dingo's howls reached them and Sabine recalled she promised to take her gun or the Aussie. Knowing the road deputy parked in a beat-up Ford Escort near the retention pond would follow her, she decided to carry her Lady Smith and Wesson. She whistled for Dingo, who tore around the corner, clearing the back fence like a pre-transgender Bruce Jenner in the 1980 Olympics high jump competition. Calvin harbored no hope of jumping that but squeezed through one of the links. Both settled in the back seat, ready for the adventure, although Sabine detected a glint of anger from Dingo. Clearly the dog wanted to drive but Sabine would not fold.

***

Sabine gave the deputy credit. He didn't crowd her or make any overt moves. She did make a mental note to tell Newt that, based on the car, all the road deputies needed a raise and quickly.

Dee surveyed the animal farm and whistled. "Sure is lonely out here."

Sabine agreed but now was not the time for philosophical discussions. "We can go around the fence past the rocks to the chimney. I don't know who to call for permission now for access to Kirby's estate but it doesn't matter. I'm not worried about trespassing charges."

The animals were safely ensconced in the Challenger with Dingo's favorite Elvis song on loud to drown the Aussie's howling, Dee and Sabine cautiously picked their way across to the chimney.

Despite two years in the elements, the structure was in excellent shape. Measuring at least ten feet across, the main fireplace was enormous. Sabine could easily walk into the opening. To the immediate right was a simple bread oven that was heated by the massive fireplace. Kirby had meticulously laid stone several yards out just as Cinnamon Wallis would have done after the Civil War to prevent accidental fire or ember jumping.

"If I were hiding something, where would I put it?" Sabine muttered out loud.

"What do you mean hiding?" A snide, cruel voice remarked.

Sabine swung around and was astounded to see Mavis Augustine in a white suit holding a very frightened Dee by the elbow with an older large caliber gun pointed at Sabine's chest.

Holding out her hands, Sabine cursed herself. Where was that damn deputy in the Ford?

"Uh, hi?" Sabine offered timidly.

"What? No snappy comeback? No venison meatball jokes?" Mavis sneered unbecomingly. The preternatural whiteness of her teeth contrasted unflattering with the orange spray tan, making Mavis resemble an angry jack o' lantern with a glowing mouth. Sabine blinked but yet the unnatural grin remained.

"I saw you." Mavis began after seeing the question in Sabine's eyes. "Little Ms. Traitor streamed the shot of you throwing a smelly shirt onto that reporter. It went viral. Congrats, Penis Snatcher, you're famous. Although you should probably do something about your hair and body. I saw everything on Facebook or should I say, "FatBook" in your case? You foolishly gave your address when you bought your small gorilla dog to the Tuxedo clinic."

Sabine clenched her fists to advance but Mavis was quicker. She tightened her grip on Dee. "Your boyfriend had the temerity to call me to let me know about the will where I get nothing. Sally Jackson is right. This is a horrid county and you're its number one citizen cretin. Kirby was fine until he started living here. He grew a conscience and someone who was desperate enough to love him. That girl with the hair worse than yours!"

"You won't get far." Sabine opted to fight back. "I had texted my boyfriend where we are and he's on the lookout for your BMW. And you're...you're not supposed to wear white during a hostage situation in October."

"Ha. You giving me fashion advice? As to your dimwitted boyfriend, all he'll find is my stupid maid trying to sell it. I gave it to her in exchange for her Ford Escort since I haven't been able to pay her full salary for a year. No loyalty in people anymore. I've been waiting all day for you to leave so I could..."

Mavis ceased talking and let loose a caterwaul worthy of an extra in a Friday the 13th sequel.

Dingo, bless her rotten heart, had rolled down the window and saw her main food female distributor in trouble and leapt onto Mavis's backside sending the socialite and her wrinkled Chanel suit into the clay. Not to be outdone, Calvin dug her kitten claws into Mavis' peroxide tresses to gouge her skull.

"Who's the gorilla now? You were beaten by a dog and a kitten. Skanky ho!" Sabine taunted. Dee kicked the gun into the chimney and was rewarded with a loud clank.

"Sit, Dingo." Sabine ordered as she pointed to Mavis' back. Dingo obliged even she was raring to run and ground her bottom into the suit while Sabine quickly dialed 911 to be connected to Gina the Gossipy Dispatcher.

"How did Dingo get out of the car?" Dee plopped onto a screaming Mavis' legs. "Sweetheart, you might as well stop struggling. There's no way you're getting my chunky tushie off you. I've been waiting two years to say this but whoever sold you the lifetime subscription to Sherwin Williams' Sunset Glow color paint did you a massive disservice. You're orange, honey. Do you understand? Your skin is orange. People are not supposed to be fluorescent orange unless they live near a Russian nuclear power plant or have a paranormal love of highlighters." She stopped for a breath.

But Dee was not finished. "And your hair. Only Marilyn Monroe had the chutzpah and facial features to pull off platinum blonde and make it look sexy.

You, Skanky Ho, are no bombshell. Hair is supposed to move naturally not like a Medusa head. Act your age!" Dee raged but turned politely to Sabine. "Thank you for the Skanky Ho comment. I had to borrow it. Can I use that from now on?"

Sabine rolled her eyes. "It's public domain so it's yours. By the way, Dingo knows how to roll down windows. I'm sure it was in the owner's manual she read."

"Smart cookie you got there." Dee cupped Dingo's face and leaned in to kiss her snout. "You are my hero."

Dingo preened like peacock and accepted the accolades as her due. Calvin continued to have a death grip on Mavis hair but Mavis, trapped under Dingo and Dee, couldn't move.

Newt's cruiser raced up to the gate. The car barely stopped before he flew out to rescue his two girls. With a few giant steps, he enveloped Sabine in a hug. Why this girl attracted trouble and excitement like a magnet was a puzzle he was both afraid and delighted to solve.

"Dee, you can get up now. I can take it from here." Newt reached to help Dee stand. "Up, Dingo, you earned your egg toaster from Sonic today." He unceremoniously yanked Mavis upright. Sabine hurriedly extricated Calvin from Mavis' hair before Newt slapped the handcuffs on her. "Maybe Ostie should hire Dingo as the new K9 officer."

Newt handed Mavis off to Dean, one of road deputies and whirled around to Sabine. "What possessed you to come out here? Here! Where we found Kirby's body? Here where you broadcast for all the world to see where the two of you two were at in the county? Dee's video is all over Facebook and has been picked up by one of the TV shows that feature viral videos."

Dee perked up. "Mavis was telling the truth? Maybe I can parlay this into publicity for the bed and breakfast!"

"That would be awesome. You could design a whole breakfast around it or...or...a tour around Jaemore County for the Weird and Stupid!" Sabine said.

Newt threw up his hands in defeat. "Where's the gun?"

"Over there." Dee motioned to the chimney. "Sabine had a great idea that maybe Kirby hid something there."

Newt ambled over to the chimney and leaned in. "I don't have time to search to prove your theory. Using his pen, he snagged the gun and held it up to the light. "It's a revolver of some sort. Old and I don't even think it's loaded. It's too rusted and I don't see any bullets in the chambers. The hammer is corroded. My guess is that it couldn't fire if it was loaded."

"Nice of Mavis to threaten us with an ancient gun. I bet she cut the brake line with a jeweled dagger to her BMW before the maid drove off." Sabine said sarcastically.

"Where's Dr. Lana?" Dee mused. "I thought they'd be together. Sort of like a rude, Botox-filled Bonnie and Clyde."

"That's one of the questions I'm going to ask Mavis. But for now, you two go to the Sheriff's office.

I'm following you so no detours for lunch at The Store or running by DFCS to pick up Mia for another batch of shenanigans. Straight to the office."

Sabine saluted. "Aye, aye. Can we stop and get a cherry Icee? And puppy treats for our heroes?"

-33-

The fight had gone out of Mavis, or maybe it was the silicone.

"When will Newt question Mavis?" Mia peered into the two-way mirror at the Sheriff's office. Dingo was curled up in the corner, sleeping with an equally exhausted Calvin.

Sabine shrugged and slurped a large Sonic Cherry Dr Pepper that Mia thoughtfully brought. It didn't matter that Sabine threatened to withhold vital gossip until she had it in her hands.

"It's been an hour." Dee commented. "Do you think we can get a hold of her mug shot? That would be prime social media information! Maybe her jumpsuit will match her skin. Or her cellmate could be a large angry woman who was betrayed by a platinum blonde as a young criminal."

Sabine was saved from answering when a decidedly more docile Mavis entered the interrogation room with the unscrupulous Hamilton Bilbo in tow. Mavis's fingers were tipped in black from the ink documenting her prints. She continuously rubbed a crumbling tissue in a vain attempt to erase the marks.

"Egads! Why'd she call him?" Mia was clearly disgusted. "Hamilton Bilbo is our local shifty graduate of the Double Talk Law School." Mia explained to Dee. "He usually represents deadbeat dads and pedophiles."

"Maybe her Buckhead attorney quit. After all, everyone's got to know she's got no money." Sabine cocked her head. "Or she paid Hamilton by....well, let's just say...in a carnal sense."

All three ladies shuddered. "Thanks, Sabine. I can't finish my strawberry slushie." Dee tossed the remainder of her drink in the garbage. "The thought of Mavis doing the horizontal hokey-pokey with anyone is going to give me nightmares. Do you think she has orange tan lines? Or does she even wear underwear? Now those are questions that's going to haunt me for a bit."

Newt strolled into the interview room and sat across from Mavis. He couldn't quite hide the look of disgust and wiped his palm after shaking Hamilton's hand.

"Ms. Augustine, I have you currently being booked for a plethora of charges. Before I turn my case over to the DA, let's go over your story. You've been read your rights at the animal farm and I personally recited them to you before you were fingerprinted."

Mavis' eyes flashed annoyance. "Why was I fingerprinted like a common criminal? Don't you have the computer touchpad where it records my prints like the rest of the civilized world? This is the most contrary, backwater marsh filled with reptilian group people who crawled their way out of the murky depths of the slimy roots of pine trees." She waved her ring finger near Newt's eyes. Sabine was happy to see the ink stubbornly clinging under her nail.

"My apologies." Newt's voice dripped with insincerity. "It's broken. Now back to the reason you're here. You drove to this county to threaten two women with an old broken gun because your late husband left you no money? What would that solve?"

"What did you do with my gun? It's an antique, handed down to me by my ancestor who fought in the Civil War. It's a rare Kerr Patent revolver made in England. I had better not see that on eBay! Or whatever goes for pawn shops here."

Newt shook his head. "You're really in no position to argue, as I'm sure Mr. Bilbo will advise you. Why, you threatened two people and I just want to know: where is Mitchell Lana?"

"Those low-class whores deserved every bit of fright. How dare they interfere with my life!" Mavis spat. "I wasn't going to do anything to them. That gun hasn't worked since before I was born. They just made me look like an idiot with my neighbors."

Newt made a notation on the case file. "Lana? Where is he?"

"Mitchell?" Mavis' puzzlement was real. "I don't know. We got into a massive fight two nights ago over the financials of the vet clinic. I traced a payment to his non-profit animal rights group called PFFT. While I applaud his concern for animals, that money should have gone to the clinic's bottom—me. I had to let my landscapers go because I was running out of money. Mr. Johnson, I don't have time to chat. When can I leave?"

"You have to be arraigned but the DA might be persuaded to go easy on you if answer a few more questions." Without waiting for an affirmative, Newt went on. "Why didn't you report your husband missing two years ago?"

Sabine noticed the fight had gone out of Mavis, or maybe it was the silicone. Whatever the reason, Mavis suddenly looked her age.

"You don't understand." Mavis murmured and then raised her voice. "The Augustines have been a fixture in Atlanta society for generations. If word got out I was penniless, I'd be shunned. I knew Kirby made a new will. The little snot even gave a copy to me when he had it signed. When he disappeared, I thought I could wait him out and sue him for abandonment or divorce. But he turned up dead. It was a sign. I hid his last will so I'd get his money."

"Were you complicit in his death?" Newt asked.

Sabine glanced at Bilbo to see if he would prevent his client from answering. Bilbo was engrossed in his smart phone, probably using county WiFi to surf porn or escort services sites.

For the second time in as many minutes, Mavis' face looked perplexed. "No. If I killed my husband,

I'd be ostracized! Men can get away with murdering people and still maintain their social status. But ladies are held to another standard. I did look into having him declared dead but the wait was unacceptable. Seven years! Someone really needs to do something about making people legally dead easier. Can't you call the governor?"

Newt refused to acknowledge that change request. "What do you know about PFFT?"

"I know Mitchell runs it. Honestly, I don't care what he does or how he convinced people to buy into his food line. He used the clinic to get rich or funnel donations and money to PFFT but my peers flocked to him. It's an old social trick. The more you treat people like they're beneath you the more people want to be your friend. Consequently, business at the clinic boomed."

Newt leaned forward in his chair to take notes on his laptop. "How did you two meet?"Mavis shrugged her bony shoulders. "I was waiting at a restaurant bar called Gatsby's on the River for a friend when Mitchell very suavely sidled up to me and bought me a drink. I'll never forget. It was Glenfiddich Janet Sheed Roberts Reserve 1955." Mavis finished dreamily as if still remembering the burn of fifty-year whiskey at $300 a glass."

Without any prompting, she continued. "We spoke about everything that night. From Singa-Sphynx Cat Rescue to my ancestry to world travels. It was a memorable evening. It was like he *knew* me. When he told me about his veterinarian degree from Brazil and how he was concerned about homeless cats, I thought fate finally handed me a partner for life."

"But you were married." Newt reminded Mavis.

A cloud of hatred descended in the room. "So? Kirby was already knee deep in this piece of crap place. We hadn't been intimate for months and I knew it was only a matter of time before Kirby divorced me and I'd get nothing. Nothing for putting up with his absences and business dinners for 17 years. I even heard about his romance with a local social climber with hair like a wild azalea bush. Little did I know Mitchell would try to double cross and try to steal from me. Mitchell told me to wait because things had a way of working out. He even vouched for me when that idiotic sheriff called two years ago asking if Kirby was around. Now I find out he only wanted to milk me for my social contacts and husband's money."

"But you didn't know where Kirby was or if he was okay! You lied your way to widowhood with a con artist!" Newt couldn't contain his anger.

"What of it?" Mavis scoffed. "I'm a victim, too. Mitchell turned out to be a swindler and stole from me. You act like I killed Kirby. I didn't, so you can't charge with me with murder."

"Not yet." Newt straightened up. "And before you insult places, you should know marshes don't contain trees. Swamps do while marshes are usually filled with grasses. Maybe your socialite knowledge may tell you how to be horrid wife and human being but at least this swamp grows genuine people who care about one another."

-34-

So sorry to ruin your plans for wedded bliss with Ms. Orange Shrew.

"What's next?" Sabine asked as she signed her typed witness statement.

Newt grimaced. "I'm working on it. I feel like I need to take a shower after dealing with that woman."

"Dee and I are going straight home. No passing 'go' or even a chocolate stop." Sabine promised. "But we'll go out to the farm when you get home. I really think there is something in the chimney."

"That's sounds good. Dean will follow you. Make sure you keep Dingo and your pistol with you. Even though there is no smoking gun that Lana killed Kirby, I feel it in my bones he had something to do with it. He's dangerous. The deputies will patrol down by the house every fifteen minutes." Newt leaned down and scratched Dingo. "You two are getting dinner from Sonic today after I finish checking Mavis into our finest suite in the jail. It's the one with a toilet and built-in in water fountain and has a window view. Every time she pees she'll moon the entire city."

Newt closed the gap between him and Sabine. "You be careful. I know you can take care of yourself but take a break from your crime solving job and be a lady of leisure tonight."

"I promise. All I want is to take a hot shower, scratch an Aussie and cuddle with a kitten." Sabine raised her right hand as if in court. Newt quickly cocooned it and kissed it softly.

***

"Sabine, how about I whip up a spinach, cheese and chicken dish for dinner? And I won't take no for an answer. Cooking calms me, and I need the calming," Dee offered in an attempt to try and steady herself from the onset of nerves.

"Dee, you won't get any protests from me. I'm so sorry that you got mixed up in this mess. Getting assaulted with a broken gun, finding out your boss is a con artist and fleeing your home. You bake or cook as much as you like." Sabine noticed the slight quiver in Dee's voice.

"Why in the Sam Hill are you apologizing?" Dee demanded. "As far as I know, you and your friends have stepped up and taken me in after everything that's happened! Deep down, I always knew Dr. Lana was a rat fink and Mavis was a fink-ette. All you did was shake me out off my rut and now I have a new life. And a cutie-patootie named Drayton who tries not to look my way but does! In fact, let's invite him to dinner. I'll get all frou-froued up and show him how gorgeous I can be."

"You don't need frou-frou to be gorgeous. And if Drayton doesn't grab you, something is wrong with him." Sabine pulled into the driveway away from the trees and acorn throwing squirrels. She waved Dean off when honked his horn as he left. Sabine wrestled with the deadbolt and the animals raced in.

"I'll see if Drayton can come if you want to get dinner started." Sabine offered. After feeding Dingo her kibble and making sure Calvin ate her kitten food, Sabine reclined into Newt's ugly orange chair. She texted Drayton an invite to dinner, muted the phone and tucked away her phone in her back pocket. She proceeded to doze with Dee humming off key in the kitchen.

Sabine was jarred awake seconds later when a deafening explosion rocked the house. Dingo was already at the front door when Sabine flung it open to view her precious Challenger burning like the gates of hell.

"WHAT THE HELL?" Sabine screamed into the flames. She hurriedly glanced around for Dingo. The dog was barking and snarling around the corner. Grabbing her leash, Sabine dashed to her dog and halted abruptly when she turned the corner.

"Shut UP!" Lana screamed and kicked Dingo in the jaw. In slow motion, Dingo flipped backwards, and her head cracked on the concrete slab. Dingo's limp body was completely still and Sabine's temper flew hotter than her burning car.

"That's my fur kid. YOU ASS! YOU FAKE VET!" Sabine launched at Lana like the Saturn V rocket from NASA. In her anger, Sabine didn't see Lana's fist before it connected with her jaw. Sabine was out for the count.

"Wakey. Wakey." Lana's singsong voice was coupled with a persistent ringing.

"Wakey. Wakey yourself, you rat bast..." Sabine started to reply but the ringing became more like bass beat from a hip-hop artist's song. She felt the hard, cool clay on her back. She squinted one eye but was met with Lana's crooked beak nose outlined in low light.

"Tsk. Tsk. Ladies don't swear." Lana smiled menacingly.

"Try this. *Eres un bastardo de rata.*" Sabine growled.

"You do understand Spanish. I thought you did when I called you *puta* at the office."

"What the hell do you want?" Sabine asked as she tested her legs and arms. Her legs moved slightly without problem but her hands were restrained with thick zip ties, resting on her stomach.

"I want to know what proof you have to bring Kirby 'justice'." Lana rocked back. "Yes, I saw your video from Facebook. Here I was getting ready to leave the country when Mavis texted me about your 15 minutes of fame."

"It seems I have you to thank, too, for finding the late, great Kirby. If you had just kept your nosy self out of my practice, Mavis and I would be married and I wouldn't have to worry about money again."

"So sorry to ruin your plans for wedded bliss with Ms. Orange Shrew."

Lana waved her comment away. "Back to the matter at hand. Why do you think Kirby is getting justice? How do you know I watched Kirby die?"

Whoa, Sabine thought silently. I wasn't expecting that. "I don't have any proof. I just wanted to piss off the TV reporter." Sabine confessed. But before her common sense could stop her, she went on. "How did Kirby die?"

"My guess would be anaphylactic shock or maybe he had a heart attack. I'm no doctor. Mavis was not pushing for divorce or money fast enough. I thought I could persuade Kirby to do a quickie divorce. I even printed off a blank divorce petition from the internet. When I pulled up, Kirby was flinging around screaming about disturbing a nest of bees. Little did he know, he dropped his EpiPen. I grabbed it and told him I'd give it if he signed it."

"But he didn't, did he, Mitchell?"

"No. He mumbled something about not being able to breathe and chased me. I thought he was going to kill me so I ran."

"With his EpiPen in your hand. Wouldn't you have thought all he wanted was his Epi-Pen and not to murder you?"

"Yes. I thought he was exaggerating his allergy. How was I supposed to know he was deathly allergic? I stopped at an oak tree and he just collapsed in front of me. His mouth and throat were swollen. Didn't even look human." Lana said distastefully as if describing a bug in his soup. "I knew I'd get blamed. Unfairly, I'm sure. I covered him up with branches and wood. I dropped the EpiPen several yards away and quietly left. Really it wasn't murder but I had just started at the Tuxedo clinic and I couldn't afford the bad publicity. It just made more sense to let people know Kirby left and never came back." Lana shifted his attention to Sabine. "Now that just leaves you, Ms. Nosy Redneck with a dead dog." Lana clasped his hands and rubbed them.

"Dingo isn't dead. If she was, she'd be up here as a ghost beating the shiznit out of you," Sabine snarled as she rolled to ease the pins and needles sensation in her legs. "Where are we?" The damp, dank, and darkness of her surroundings did not connect with anyplace she could identify as being in Greenleaf or Jaemore County. The coolness of the temperature brought a prickling of goose bumps to her skin.

"You don't recognize it? It's the cellar of the place Kirby was restoring on his farm. Kind of stupid if you ask me. The past needs to stay in the past. Why throw money after an old cabin?" Lana stood and paced the large area.

Sabine felt her back pocket vibrate. She searched her brain for the reason. Did Lana put a vibrator in her pocket? Then she recalled. Her cell phone was muted but still alerted her for notifications. Surely Dee called the fire department and Newt once she found out Sabine was gone. Then her heart constricted. What if Dee came outside and Lana killed her?

Knowing Newt would trace her cell made Sabine breathe easier. She had objected and was offended when Newt insisted on using one of those track your people apps on her phone. He had been insistent on it after the narrow escape from the Lindy Mills incident. Now, she was glad he had been beyond persistent, into demanding. This knowledge of Newt being able to track her location did not bring relief to her fear for Dee and Dingo, though.

"Did you free all the animals on the farm because you were opposed to Kirby supplying meat?" Sabine asked.

Mitchell smirked. "No, I didn't. I don't have problems eating meat. Being a fruitarian or whatever crap is hot now, is just my way of fitting into society. I don't give a crap about how restaurants get their meat. People can line up and take a baseball bat to kill chickens for all I care. Hell, if I had a bat when your mangy mutt came at me, I'd have whacked her brains out. Celebrities are all about helping animals now and I'm just along for the ride."

Sabine shook with fury. "You burned my car, hit my dog, and now kidnapped me. You better hope I don't get loose 'cause I will open up a can of whoop ass on you the world has never seen."

"Oh, quit blustering. You and I both know you won't get free and you'll probably die down here. I can't leave a loose end like you while I head off to wherever I want."

"Sure you can. Just walk away." Sabine encouraged him. "But tell me more about your PFFT scam."

“What do you want to know?” Mitchell almost perked up and puffed his chest out with pride.

“How did you target Mavis?”

“The newspaper is so valuable for this.” Mitchell commented. “So is the internet but the number one way to choose a target is go with your gut. I have great instincts and can think on my feet.”

“Props for you for that.” Sabine complimented. “To be good in any job, you need to fake it till you make it.”

“Yes, that’s exactly it.” Mitchell squatted back down. “I think we’re more alike that anyone thinks.”

Sabine swallowed a nasty vurp that threatened to spill forth. “Yeah. Yeah. I see that too. Tell me about how you got out here. Uber?”

“Uber?” No one in their right mind could be paid enough to drive out to this God-forsaken area. I simply broke into an old Saturn. You were too stupid to realize that you gave your address. All I had to do was wait for you to leave without that annoying cop boyfriend of yours. I know a bit of chemistry and can construct an effective Molotov cocktail thanks to my days in Mexico working for a coyote. Do you know what a coyote is?” Lana asked.

“Yes, it’s a smuggler who, for a very high fee, sneaks undocumented and desperate people into the US usually through the desert or other dangerous path.” After meeting meth dealer Lindy Mills last spring, Sabine thought she had found the most horrendous person in the world but Lana might just topple Lindy from the top spot as the devil’s concubine.

"Wow, that's very good." Mitchell nodded as if he was an elementary school teacher. "You and Dee going into cahoots was a bit of bad luck. Are you two together? Do you swing both ways?" When Sabine refused to answer, he continued. "Dee was all too familiar with my car so I had to improvise. That's okay. I hated that Prius. But God forbid an eco-warrior drive a luxury car or even a truck. First thing I'm going to get is a sports car. Maybe in red."

While Mitchell was daydreaming about a 'Stang Shelby XLT in Ruby Red with 500 horsepower, Sabine glimpse a thin beam of light to the right. She even detected a faint rustle. The good guys were here!

The scraping became louder and interrupted Mitchell's daydream. "What is that noise?"

Sabine cleared her throat. "It's a possum. When I was out here the other day, I saw a momma possum with four little ones clinging to her. They're usually nocturnal so..." She trailed off, praying that Mitchell wouldn't investigate until Newt was in a position to act.

"Nasty animals....wait. October isn't breeding season for possums. I lived in Mexico for a few years so I know. You're lying."

"No, I'm not." Sabine denied quickly. "Possums breed any time. My major at Texas A&M was...was...marsupial studies."

"Was not."

"Was too."

"I'm going to check it out anyway." Mitchell heaved himself up and was soon swallowed up by the darkness.

A strident screech of pain echoed in the cellar. A small animal darted out and shot toward Sabine.

"Hey, Mr. Possum or whatever you are. I'm a friendly here. No need to spray me or bite." Sabine nervously whispered.

A light blinked in her face and Sabine was relieved to recognize Snookie and her solar powered light collar. Snookie immediately licked Sabine's face and wagged her wienie tail in bliss. In the background, the screeching became moans.

Over the moans and Snookie's excited whining, Sabine detected Newt calling out her name. It was faint at first but got stronger the closer he got to Sabine. It hurt Sabine to recognize the worried and scared tone in his voice.

"I'm down in the cellar with Snookie. Mitchell Lana is somewhere down here, moaning. Not sure if it's a pleasurable mating call or what. I don't think he has a gun and I'm tied up."

If Sabine lived to a hundred, she'd never forget the sight of her boyfriend leaping into the pit like a Scandanavian Superman with thinning blonde hair. Seconds later four more deputies slid down the steep embankment. They followed Mitchell's moans quickly but with extreme caution.

"My God. You're safe. You're safe." Newt framed Sabine's face and kissed her long and deep. "I've never been more scared in my entire life when I heard the 911 call." He whipped out his Swiss army knife and cut the zip ties on her wrists. "Thank God, you had your cell phone and that track your people app.

"Lana kicked Dingo in the jaw and she busted her head on the concrete slab. Is she okay?"

"Yes. Dee called 911 when she heard the explosion and saw you shoot out after Dingo. Dee said Dingo needed to get a vet. She's afraid Dingo has a concussion. I gave her Dr. Emberly's information. She and Drayton are on their way to the clinic now with Dingo."

"Are you sure? You're not just making things up to calm me."

"No, *Älskling*. Dingo will be back ruling the roost tomorrow." With reluctance, Newt extricated himself. "I am going to deal with Lana. Lee will be here and I suspect the Wallises also." Newt called Dean and ordered him wait with Sabine and to keep an eye on Snookie.

"Where is she? Where is my sister?" Mia shouted shrilly. "You have no right, Ostie. I'm her comfort person. It's the law. Look it up. We're not a hoity-toity airline where you can stop a federally protected program like therapy animals. You can't deny someone their therapeutic comfort object or animal."

"It's okay, Mia. I'm coming up and I have Snookie" Sabine leaned heavily on a deputy to climb out of the pit.

"Baby girl." Mrs. Wallis pushed past and enveloped Sabine in a bear hug. Sabine inhaled the Jean Nate splash. Mrs. Wallis favored and savored the attention and love. Cheers from the large rubber-necking crowd from the county surrounded them.

Sabine dimly recognized the booing from the citizens when they witnessed a moaning Mitchell

Lana being hauled from the cellar strapped to an EMS gurney. His left leg immobilized with a splint.

"Oh, quit your whining." Andy Paulsen, one of the EMTs, shook the gurney, causing Mitchell to groan more.

Several local delinquents began a barrage of rotting tomatoes and eggs onto Lana. Elvis Lyons even tossed the remnants of fish bait from Master Baits with Maxi Masters giving pointers on their aim. Melvin Thomas braved his ophidiophobia and threw a small garter snake which landed on Mitchell's neck. Everyone laughed uproariously because Mitchell was strapped down and could not remove the snake or fish guts.

"Stay out of Jaemore County!" Maxi hollered. "We don't want your crap!"

"You kick a dawg or a cat again, ya ain't getting' back up." Edweener threatened. "Your ass will be grass and I'll be John Deere."

"Let me look at you in the light." Mia shifted her head. "You'll have a slight bruise on your jaw. That can be covered by makeup. He hits like a little girl. You have a good size lump on your forehead."

Sabine thrust Snookie into Mia's arms. "Snookie's a hero. Lana heard her in the cellar. I don't why she was there but he went to check on her and from the looks of it, he hurt himself in the dark."

"*Ja*, she is the hero." Newt reached and scratched the dachshund's ears. "She was digging a hole and Lana stepped right into it. He has a compound fracture. Serves the jerk right."

"Snookie saved the day! She deserves some sort of police medal." Mia hooted excitedly. Snookie looked unimpressed and promptly fell asleep.

Newt smiled. "That she does. She's getting Sonic for a week compliments of the sheriff's office."

Once the ambulance left the vicinity, the crowd started to disperse. Many Greenleafers promised to deliver food for the rest of the month to help in Sabine's recovery.

Sabine begged off a visit to the hospital and stubbornly insisted on visiting the animal hospital to care for Dingo. Newt patiently listened and vetoed all plans that didn't include Sabine going straight to bed. He did call Dee and Drayton who both volunteered to stay overnight with Dingo at Doc Emberly's office to monitor Dingo. Sabine was happy to hear Dingo was awake and had already scared the other animals into cowering in the corner of their cages. With that last bit of information, Sabine fell asleep before leaving the scene.

-35-

Tales from Edweener's fictitious prison life in South Georgia.

Sabine stretched and winced. Her arms were achy, and her swollen jaw locked up. It was 11:00 a.m. and her stomach grumbled. When she reached the living room, Mia was sitting cross-legged on the couch with several DFCS files and her laptop. Calvin and Shadow were curled up on the top of a velour pillow decorated in Shadow's signature colors of pink and lavender.

"Hey!" Sabine's throat was raw and hurt to even grunt.

"Hey back. Newt's at the office, finishing writing reports, booking or interviewing Mavis or Mitchell Lana or something. He said he'd be late and asked me to spend the day with you. Dad suggested waterboarding the fake vet but Newt reminded him of that pesky 8th amendment of the Bill of Rights—the one outlawing cruel and unusual punishment."

Mia shoved the laptop off her lap and motioned for Sabine to sit. "Momma sent potlikker and cornbread over."

"I don't eat potlikker."

"I know that and she knows that. She sent milk gravy and biscuits over along with a vat of sweet tea and Granny Lureen's hot chocolate mix. Momma thought you might need something soft after that rat fink hit you. I'll heat it up."

Calvin roused herself and arched her back. She leapt on Sabine's lap and purred happily. Mia returned loaded down with food. "You eat and I'll tell you everything."

Sabine was amazed at the quickness of events. After Lana was transported to the hospital for treatment of the broken leg, Newt posted a deputy to watch over him. Lana was not arrested yet because Newt didn't want the county to be liable for any medical bills. Mavis broke down after a night in county lockup.

It seemed Edweener decided that Mavis needed a special brand of justice, Jaemore County style. Using her husband's keys, Edweener "incarcerated" herself in the cell next to Mavis. All through the night, she regaled Mavis with tales from Edweener's fictitious prison life in South Georgia. The breakfast of lumpy oatmeal, stale toast and weak coffee was the last straw. Mavis offered to cop to a lesser charge in exchange for a reduction in charges and to testify against her former paramour.

To everyone's dismay, the Feds showed up bright and early both at the jail and the hospital. News of Mitchell Lana's charity scam reached their ears and the Internal Revenue Service swiftly brought tax evasion charges. They swooped in like vultures and asserted federal jurisdiction. The IRS was not the only government agency after Lana. The Food and Drug Administration, the Federal Trade Commission and the US Department of Agriculture all wanted a piece of Lana. Drayton had passed the dog treats from Dr. Lana's Complete Companion Sustenance line that Sabine bought to a few friends at the University of Georgia labs. Dee's suspicions were confirmed. It was indeed another dog food already on the market that was repackaged and repriced. After Lana paroled out of the federal prison and other agencies, Jaemore County and the rest of the Metro Atlanta law enforcement could imprison him.

"The worst part about the Feds is that we had a lottery going on for people to win seats on the jury for the trial. People were paying up to $50 to enter. Melvin Thompson said he'd do free tattoos for the judge for life if he was put on the jury." Mia pouted. "Daddy was making plans to impersonate a bailiff and MeeMaw offered to add laxatives to any meals that Lana ate at the jail. After he was found guilty, we had a festival and parade all planned to send him off covered in rotting food."

"Where's Mavis going?" Sabine let the last gravy-ful biscuit slide down her throat.

"The Feds took her, too. They ruined everything." Mia seethed.

A familiar snarl outside the front door signaled the end of the conversation. Mia flung open the door allowing Dingo to race in with Dee in tow. Jumping on Sabine was the next order of business followed by a frantic face licking by both the dog and Calvin.

"She got so excited when Dr. Emberly released her. It was like she knew what he was saying." Dee said. "I couldn't hold her back any longer."

Sabine giggled as she concentrated on scratching Dingo's underside. "That's fine. I've always said Dingo is smarter than most humans. If she had thumbs, she'd be unstoppable. Now she has Calvin as a minion, I think the Secret Service needs to be notified."

Drayton filled the front doorway with a large garbage filled with items. "Dingo has her admirers. At least thirty people dropped off dog biscuits and toys for her. Say what you will about rural Georgia, we're a loyal bunch who care about each other including our pets. And for you, Edweener dropped off a bottle of something that smells like rubbing alcohol so it's probably her white lightnin'."

"How are feeling?" Drayton sat the bag down. Dingo and Calvin raced to it sniffing around it.

"I'm good." Sabine nodded. "I'm just achy."

"Lee gave me the day off so I can drive you to the doctor or...." He grimaced "Or I can take you to look at new cars."

A stream of expletives spewed from Sabine's mouth. "I totally forgot about the Challenger. Is it still outside?" She flew up with her fists clenched.

"No." Drayton looked fearful. "Newt had it towed for evidence. Sabine, I saw it. It's a total loss.

I'm sorry. Newt's looking into a way that Lana's seized money can buy you a new car."

"Shopping?" Mia piped in. "Let's go shopping. Car shopping no less!"

"No. I want to go back to the chimney and see if there's a hiding spot." Sabine decided.

"We'll all go." Dee chimed. "And we'll carry your gun, a baseball bat, some pepper spray, and my newly bought taser."

"And if anyone messes with us, I'll make sure they'll never find a place to live here." Mia vowed.

It was a decidedly better trip to the farm. Sabine refused to peer into the cellar but instead concentrated on the task at hand.

"From what I recall, the hidey hole would be on the front side near the baking oven. Not too hot to burn anything delicate but still in the stones for protection.

Mia cocked her head. "Do you hear that? It sounds like someone crying."

Dee stuck her head around the chimney. "Oh. Hello! I'm Dee. Are you okay?"

"Who is she talking to?" Mia mouthed silently to Sabine.

Sabine shrugged her shoulders and followed Dee. A heartbroken Lottie McCall was leaning up against the stones with spent tissues littering the ground around her.

"Sabine Metzke, I don't want to talk to you. Get your nosy butt out of my business. That guy should have kicked you around before they rescued you." Despite her grief, Lottie managed to sound haughty and cruel.

"Sabine!" Drayton called. "I found something."

With that pronouncement, all the ladies crowded around Drayton who had picked a loose stone that was cleverly camouflaged as a cabinet pull. A second later, Drayton pulled out a hidden drawer revealing a plastic bag. The bag held a small chamois tie string bag.

"Should we?" He asked.

Sabine nodded. When Drayton poured the contents of the chamois bag into his hands, Lottie inhaled and hiccupped simultaneously. A small diamond ring and a delicate necklace twinkled in the sunlight.

"Those were Kirby's mother's things. This is all your fault, Sabine. If you had never stuck your nose in everyone's business, I'd never know Kirby suffered so much before he died. I never really knew how he felt about me." This renewed a fresh sobbing fit from Lottie. This proved too much for Lottie and she raced off to a small copse of trees and over brush.

Dee looked affronted. "That's kind of rude. All we wanted to do was help."

"Yeah. That's Lottie for you." Sabine replied dryly. "We better go find her. She'd get attacked by rabid raccoons and blame us."

They discovered Lottie leaning up against a rock, crying. Branches had torn off in her hair making Lottie look more and more like the Bob Ross Chia Pet.

"She's not a pretty crier." Mia whispered to Sabine.

While Sabine privately agreed, she didn't think it was the time to comment on the monstrosity of Lottie's appearance.

"Lottie." Mia stepped forward. Sabine was amazed to hear a note of concern in her best friend's voice. Either Mia had been taking acting lessons from Dame Helen Mirren or Lottie's grief had penetrated their long-held feud between the two.

"Lottie." Mia repeated. "Kirby left you his mother's diamond ring and necklace to you according to his will so he did....he was...oh, heck, he had feelings for you."

From that announcement, Sabine determined that Helen Mirren was in town and coaching Mia.

"Really?" Lottie raised hopeful eyes at Mia.

"Yes. Drayton is the executor of the will. I'm not sure when you'd get them but you should know at least one person cared about you." Mia reluctantly admitted. "Is that right, Drayton?"

There was silence. "Drayton?" Mia asked again.

"Mia, how much do you know about this land?" Drayton murmured as if awed.

"Not much. This was Glenda Dupont's land before the Civil War. Daddy said Glenda was killed when she was working for the Underground Railroad. Cinnamon Wallis was her best friend and a freed slave. Glenda specifically gave this land to Cinnamon. During the 1920's, we had a drought or something and Cinnamon's grandchildren gave up farming. It's just been handed down through our family. Why?"

"This is actually a cemetery. Lottie is leaning up against a tombstone. It's Cinnamon Wallis' headstone. Mia, this is your ancestors' resting place!"

"No way!" Mia shoved Lottie from the headstone and read the faded carving. "Cinnamon Wallis. 1829-1899. Beloved wife, mother and friend. May the Lord hold her and descendants in the palm of His loving hands."

Sabine brushed off another tombstone nearby. "Jedidiah Wallis. 1825-1888. Beloved husband of Cinnamon."

Lottie crinkled her nose. "Did your ancestor marry her brother? Because it all makes sense now. The Wallis family is full of inbreeding."

"No, Lottie. You're wrong." Sabine defended. "After the Civil War, most ex-slaves didn't have last names so they named themselves after famous people like Lincoln, their former owners or someone they admired. I'd be willing to bet that Jedidiah was a former slave and they decided to name themselves after a heroic and brave woman."

Drayton's exuberance was contagious. Even Lottie joined in pulling kudzu and broken branches from the clearing. Before long, Sabine counted seven graves in various states of disarray. Most of the headstones were weathered and the ones that were readable told the story of four deaths in 1872 of an unknown epidemic. All four were for younger children.

"Think of the history!" Drayton exclaimed. "And thanks to Kirby, we can restore this land as a monument to perseverance and friendship. All because of Cinnamon's loyalty, love and dedication."

"Jolly Black Giant, it sounds like you're not really a Wallis." Lottie said nastily to Mia. Clearly the truce had ended.

-36-

So far, World War III had not broken out.

"Dingo! Don't you dare jump into that pond and get poop all over you," Sabine warned her dog. She and Mia were sitting at Winkie Park finishing up an order of chili cheese fries. Sabine grimaced when a goose launched a poop attack over her new truck. The ink of the loan for her Ram was barely dry and a bird was already soiling it.

"Relax," Mia chided. "It's a beautiful Saturday evening and you can wash the poo off."

"Too bad our significant others were too busy for us." Sabine whined and then shivered. Fall weather strolled late and it was now only a week before Thanksgiving. She still had much to do before Newt's parents flew in from Sweden in a few days. Calvin had taken to sleeping on Newt's chest at night which forced Dingo to sleep on Sabine's feet.

"Newt just has to finish up the paperwork on Mitchell Lana. And Lee is interviewing replacements for fire educator since Drayton quit."

Lana was a guest in a federal prison at an unknown location still recovering from the broken leg. Mavis pled to a few misdemeanor charges. She was warned never to step foot into Jaemore County again—an order she accepted with alacrity.

Life was returning to normal. Dee had bought Matilda Jaemore's house and was in the process of securing licenses and remodeling the land and the house to her vision of a bed and breakfast named the Greenleaf Garden Inn. Drayton rarely left her side on the weekend, taking control of the landscaping to ensure the "garden" part of the name rang true.

Drayton also had his hands full during the work week learning about his new job as executive director of the Morgan Historical Restoration Foundation. He set up several ambitious projects and was pushing himself to open the farm to the public in December. His first task was to hire Mr. Wallis as Project Manager to restore the Wallis homestead. Mrs. Wallis had pleaded and bribed Drayton with homemade lemon bars to give Mr. Wallis a productive job instead of binge-watching crime shows and training Snookie to be a K9 officer. Mr. Wallis was training to be the Homestead's first tour guide. In a fit of compassion, Drayton also hired Lottie as an events coordinator to establish the farm as a destination wedding/party option.

One of the more sobering days was Kirby's funeral. The First Baptist Church hosted the event and Drayton gave a moving eulogy. Internment was at the right of Cinnamon Wallis' grave. Sabine thought that was a fitting spot for a man who learned the value of history and friendship from the Wallis' land.

Sally Jackson from Channel 7 deigned not to cover the story and rumor had it that her office had moved to the basement of the television station due to the lingering pungent skunk odor in her hair.

Lottie and Matilda had moved into a house one street over in the Wallis' neighborhood. So far, World War III had not broken out, but there was a pool at The Store with times and dates and location of the first battle. Sabine hoped it would occur before she and Newt flew out to Texas for Thanksgiving. She even started a rumor that Lottie and Old Lady Hughes had become best friends. Mia's only reaction was an angry tic above her left eye.

"Let's go back to your house. Your mom was making a final batch of red velvet cookies for the last blackmail payment to Drayton." Sabine brightened. Mrs. Wallis' cookies, like the rest of her kitchen magic, was not to be missed.

"No. I want to finish these fries." Mia stuffed more chili in her mouth.

The stillness was pierced by a police siren. Newt's cruiser swung and skidded into the parking lot. Sabine's thoughts raced as she pictured Mitchell Lana escaping in a revamped hi-tech wheelchair.

Mr. Wallis jumped out the passenger seat and bubbled with happiness. Newt followed. Mrs. Wallis banged on the divider in the back seat. She looked a little queasy after Newt freed her.

"What did Mr. Wallis do to earn this?" Sabine grinned. Then she glanced around and had an intense feeling of déjà vu.

Newt in his court suit knelt in front of Sabine. Dingo stood and stared at Sabine intently. The park was filled to the brim with neighbors and friends. "Sabine Anne Metzke, you drive me crazy; you make me laugh and most of all, you make life worth living for me. Will you and Dingo marry me?"

In Newt's hands was a stunning princess cut diamond ring. He removed it gently. "This ring has been handed down in my family. The diamond was given to my great grandmother as a tribute by a Dutch Jewish family who her son rescued from the Nazis in 1942. He died helping them. The oldest child of each generation receives it to give to his bride."

Sabine couldn't speak. The sunset was framing the gorgeous ring. The diamond blinked and the moment in time stopped.

Dingo impatiently nudged her and Sabine found herself nodding yes. As the newly engaged couple kissed, incessant barking put an end to the moment.

Elvis Lyons strolled-up holding a squirming Snookie and a femur bone. "Miss Mia, she did it. Snookie dug up Dorcas Priest."

Made in the USA
Columbia, SC
25 November 2019